WHERE CURLEWS CRY

As a solicitor in the small northern mining town of Hexham, Sam Browne knows more than most about the affairs of many of the town's inhabitants. He has known several of his clients – men such as Michael McIver and Tom Beardsley – since his schooldays, and he has become a friend of their families. When tragedy strikes, affecting the different families in different and terrible ways, Sam finds himself unwillingly drawn into the complicated emotional entanglements of their lives...

WHERE CURLEWS CRY

by

Elizabeth Gill

Magna Large Print Books
Long Preston, North Yorkshire,
BD23 4ND, England.

British Library Cataloguing in Publication Data.

Gill, Elizabeth
    Where curlews cry.

A catalogue record of this book is available from the British Library

ISBN   0-7505-2412-X

First published in Great Britain in 2004 by Severn House Publishers Ltd.

Copyright © 2004 by Elizabeth Gill

Cover illustration © Len Thurston by arrangement with P.W.A. International

The moral right of the author has been asserted

Published in Large Print 2005 by arrangement with Severn House Publishers Ltd.

Magna Large Print is an imprint of Library Magna Books Ltd.

Printed and bound in Great Britain by T.J. (International) Ltd., Cornwall, PL28 8RW

One

The weather was cold and already there had been snow in Hexham. The elegant Georgian houses had white window sills and all around the Abbey, with its stained-glass windows that shone sapphire and ruby in the morning sunshine, people trod carefully through the slush.

It was market day and the town was busy. Sam Browne, local solicitor, was sitting in his office in the street called Robson's Field. The houses in this street were all on one side, some with gardens so luxuriant that trees hung over the walls on the steep hill. Some of the walls had gates, behind which there were narrow lanes and neat yards and, in summer, pots of herbs and flowers spilled over on to the flags and families sat in shaded gardens, completely secluded, only moments from the town.

The building which housed Sam's business was inside one of those gates, a house almost two hundred years old, with stout walls, generous rooms and a big garden, the gate itself half hidden by the trees which overhung the garden. But it was well known to the townspeople, since Sam's mother and father had both been in the practice and had lived there before they grew prosperous and moved into the country, to a fortified farmhouse where Sam and his twin brother, Dominic, had grown up.

Both of Sam's parents had died a long time ago and Dominic had been ill most of his life and had died the previous Christmas. Sam was thirty-five, divorced, no children, not bad-looking in a northern kind of way, with sharp cheekbones and keen eyes, the kind of eyes which in former times had stood the Northumbrians in good stead as they watched over their sheep and cattle, mined their lead and coal and minded their farms and families. Sam was thin, with the kind of thinness which meant that he didn't think much about food, and he was six feet tall. His ancestors had thankfully been much shorter, to go down pits and hew coal and into quarries and lead mines.

That particular morning he had been busy and was glad to get back to the office. He had had two difficult encounters already and it was not yet noon. The first was that he had had to visit Edward West, who owned a drift mine called the Sunny Mary, a few miles beyond the town. The mine provided work for almost all the people who lived in the village of Burnside, a settlement which was nothing but a few streets on a hill with a church at the top, a chapel at the bottom and the fells all around.

Mr West had been his father's client, had been with them for as long as Sam could remember. He was in his sixties and was ill. He had had cancer on and off for years but this time Sam could see he was not going to get better.

Sam knew the family well, had gone to primary school with the son, Stephen, before they each went off to different public schools. The Wests had been prosperous people; they lived in one of the biggest houses around Hexham, Allenheads House, situated in its own grounds almost equi-distant between Hexham and Burnside. The West family had brought coal from there for almost a hundred years.

The last few years had been hard, the mine was not prospering, it was cheaper to bring it in from other countries and, to the dismay of the locals, Polish coal was brought in through northern ports to supply local needs. The downward turn in business showed in the Wests' house, Sam thought.

There was no central heating. Edward West lay upstairs with a coal fire for comfort. Although it might have looked romantic to other people, there was very little which pleased about having to lug coal up a big flight of stairs. They had no help nor could afford any and Mrs West did everything herself.

The house had an orchard, a kitchen garden, a front garden with formal beds, a rockery and a big oblong rose bed, a pond behind it with a paddock, a circular drive at the front of the house. The house itself had a great hall with stained-glass windows in an arch halfway up the stairs. It had a back stairs too and a back kitchen and a dairy and a wash house and all the things people had needed in the late nineteenth century when the Empire meant that middle-class people were prosperous and servants were cheap to employ.

Sam knew the house well from his childhood and teenage years. The bedrooms were too large for comfort and the bathroom was cavernous. The windows were flaking paint and many of them were draughty and, he suspected, rotten. The carpets were thin and inadequate and the curtains, most of which were velvet, reflected the fact that they had gone through many a summer, so worn and faded were they. The furniture was dusty and, although it was old, it was not the kind of old which would have got it into any of the antique shops in the area. The windows were flecked with rain and dirt and most of the house was freezing.

Mrs West wore a lot of clothes. She was a proud woman and Sam dared not suggest to her that the social services might be able to help. Did Stephen not know how his parents were living? He had stayed in London after university and had become a top journalist, working for a quality newspaper. Sam knew that they had been disappointed in his marriage. Susan West was beautiful, she had been a model, from a modest background, and Sam could remember having heard that Mrs West said nothing was ever good enough for a woman who had nothing. After they were married Susan West gave up modelling, did no work of any kind and did not produce children, so she was doubly condemned by her in-laws.

It had been a difficult meeting this morning in Mr West's bedroom, Sam's front was scorched by the fire, his back freezing against the draught. Stephen, Sam thought, must be told how ill his father was and he must come home.

Sam didn't envy Stephen's homecoming. Since his marriage, he had rarely come back. Sam had heard rumours that the mine was badly managed since Mr West had been so ill, and was losing a great deal of money. The word bankruptcy had been mentioned. If Stephen West didn't come back soon, there might be nothing for him to come back to. Mr West had been gradually making his possessions over to his wife so that it would be solely hers before he died and there would be as little tax to pay as possible.

Sam made comforting noises, took details and went back to the office. He drove through the town. The shops were already getting in goods for Christmas. Sam didn't want Christmas to come, it would remind him of last year. Dominic had been so ill throughout the bad weather in early December and Sam had had to go and leave him most days with a nurse until the last fortnight or so. His brother had died on Boxing Day.

Sam's memories of Dominic were most difficult early in the mornings when it was dark at the farm. He would hear the wind outside, rushing across the open fell, and also the noise his ears had become accustomed to over the years, the sound of his twin brother getting out of bed. It didn't matter what light there was or what the season, how cold the house, whether the curtains were drawn or not, Dominic awoke every day of his life at exactly half past five.

At one time Sam had tried to alter things, getting Dominic to stay up later so that he would be tired and sleep in, but he never did. If Dominic had gone to bed at four he would still get up at the same time.

For almost as long as Sam could remember, the routine had been the same. The house was his brother's safety and his life. He had lived there since he was small and knew nothing else and he was happy there. During the week he would go to the day centre. Otherwise he would stay here, mostly with Sam. He would come into Sam's room, hair ruffled with sleep, pyjamas creased.

'Is today Sunday?'

'No, it's Wednesday.'

Dominic didn't wait. He went off to the bathroom. Within half an hour he would be washed and dressed, having his breakfast and watching his favourite cartoons on television.

He always had the same thing for breakfast, porridge in his special bowl. Sam would drop him off at the day centre and then go on to work, so Sam was always at work long before anybody else, and it was the best time of the day. With nobody about, he could think and sometimes he accomplished more work in those two hours than he did all day, but it meant a long day. In the evenings he would fall asleep over the television.

Sam picked his way across the marketplace now, thinking that his secretary, Kathleen, would make some coffee as soon as he got in. He hadn't far to go, just past the old gaol and halfway down the hill. There were a great many people whom Sam recognized and several whom he spoke to and others who nodded and waved. It made him feel better, knowing that he was among friends. Apart from the time at school, he had lived here all his life. As he set off down the hill, his blue eyes caught sight of someone he hadn't expected to see, Michael McIver, a few years older than him. Michael had done well for himself. His father had been a pit-man at the Sunny Mary but Michael was a chemist. He worked for a big American company which was based in Germany. It made cosmetics, toiletries. It had an office in

Newcastle and Michael had worked there first.

'Mike!' he yelled and the other man turned. Sam's business had made him particularly sensitive to people's problems and Michael didn't look glad to see him or pleased to be seen. 'Thought you were in Frankfurt,' Sam said.

'I am, just home for ... you know.'

Sam didn't know.

'On business?' he said.

'Yes.'

Michael was always cagey, Sam thought. He didn't know why, and for the past year or two Gareth Forester, Sam's partner, had dealt with Michael's legal affairs, so Sam had no idea what Michael was doing there but his instincts told him something was wrong.

There was something about his stance, his whole body, which spoke of defeat. Sam could see through people as though they had no skin, blood, muscle or bone, and he had known Michael for a long time. Michael's shoulders went down.

'They let me go in August,' he said. 'Why do I always tell you things?' He looked away, at other people, at the wet street and beyond, where the oranges, pears and apples on the stall were rounds of colour in the grey day.

'Does this mean you haven't told anybody else?'

Michael looked at him again.

'Caroline thinks I'm doing well,' he said.

'You'll get something else soon. You're clever, you've got experience, qualifications.'

'I'm forty-five. That's old in this game.'

Michael was married to a beautiful woman, red hair, green eyes, endless legs. They had a daughter, Victoria, who was seventeen. He had a lot, Sam thought, he was lucky. No empty bed, no echoing rooms.

'You will. How's Caroline?'

'She's at her mother's.'

Sam hesitated.

'You should tell her,' he advised.

'I promised myself I'd always keep her well. Her parents never thought I was good enough for her. Anyway, I have an interview this week in London. It's not as good as the job I lost but it will have to do, if I get it.'

Sam tried to cheer him but had to get back. He had another appointment at midday.

Kathleen made him some coffee. Even through the closed window of his office Sam could hear people walking into town up the steep hill and into the pubs. He had to wait for his client. Usually it was the other way round, he often made people wait, not deliberately, just because the law was complex and so were people, but Tom Beardsley was late.

Tom was another man whom Sam had known for a long time. Tom was American. He had come to Hexham to live with his grandmother when his parents split up. He was a teenager then. Tom was not, Sam reflected, what English people thought of when they thought of Americans. Tom was the old-style eastern American, in that he came from well-heeled Connecticut. Tom was educated, well mannered, softly spoken. His parents had divorced, his mother had gone off and not been heard of since and then his father had died and left him a great deal of money. Sam had met Tom fairly often socially over the years. Tom, like Michael, lived in Frankfurt, they had worked for the same company for years. Tom was a sales director.

They rarely met in a business capacity, so Sam was curious and not quite comfortable that Tom wanted to see him that morning. Tom was the kind of person Sam liked best, in that he looked after himself. He had long since made his will, had made sound financial investments for himself and his young wife. He was clever, successful and shrewd. Sam liked that. It was a solicitor's dream that your client came to you for sensible things but he could not imagine what was bringing Tom to him that morning.

It was afternoon, twenty-five past twelve. There was no other appointment until two o'clock, Sam had been hoping they could go to the pub and have a sandwich and a pint and talk about things which had nothing to do with legal matters, since they hadn't seen each other in months. He went to the window and looked out over the big yard and the tubs of flowers which greeted his clients at the back of the house and up further at the surrounding houses. Beyond them it would be a bright day on the moors and he was restless. The door opened and Kathleen, a pretty woman of thirty whom Sam had lately suspected of trying to get pregnant and leave him for domesticity, opened the door, smiling.

'Mr Beardsley,' she said.

Tom wore a silver-grey suit and a generous smile but Sam was undeceived. Too many people had walked in at that door with a similar strained look in their eyes. Something was wrong and all Tom's instant American apologies would not mend it. Sam's heart sank. What was it? Tom had married a lovely girl, he had a good job, money, brains, prospects, charm.

The door closed. Sam went forward and shook his hand, slightly formal because he realized that this was not a trivial matter and there would be no friendly pub drink and sandwich.

'Tom, have a seat,' he said. 'How's Jess?'

Jess Beardsley was the most beautiful woman ever to come out of Burnside Village. She was twenty-four, looked like people imagined orphans looked, with huge dark eyes, freckles and a lot of glossy hair. She was tall, slender and softly spoken. A great many people envied Tom Beardsley his wife. He stopped apologizing for his lateness, sat down and didn't look at Sam for several moments, always a bad sign. Sam didn't say anything, he believed in letting people say what they had to say in their own time. Misery was a common thing in a solicitor's office, so was joy and despair and unsolved problems. After a while Tom looked up, met Sam's carefully blank eyes.

'I'm going to leave my wife,' he said.

Only Sam's training kept his mouth shut

and his expression level.

'I want you to sort things out,' Tom said quickly as though the very words hurt. 'She'll get half, of course, I'm not trying to cheat her of anything and I know it's my fault. I'll want a divorce. You can put things in motion.'

There was somebody else, Sam knew. Women left men for all kinds of reasons but men only left women when they had found somebody else. Sam also realized that Tom hadn't told her yet. Also that Tom and Jess's marriage had been something he relied on, believed in, was glad of. It had been something to hold on to in your mind on a particularly bad day. Jess held Tom's hand at parties as though he was too precious to leave her sight. She would smile into his eyes. Jess adored Tom and she was gentle and kind. She had the warmest gaze that Sam had ever seen and it was for her husband only.

'It's none of your business,' Tom said sharply. In the silence he got up. 'It isn't anything to do with you.' He turned his back, pushed his hands into his trouser pockets in a way that would have made any decent tailor shudder.

'Did I say anything?'

'Goddamn you, you don't have to! You were born to be a bloody solicitor, sitting there, saying nothing and judging people. I've met a woman who's my intellectual and social equal. Jess is neither of those things. She bores me.' His voice was rough, guilty. 'She's always there, always waiting for me. She never has a bad day, the house is perfect, the meals are perfect, she's perfect, so eager to please, so...' He stopped, looked down at what had been a pretty carpet twenty years ago and was now indistinguishable in colour.

'You have to tell her,' Sam said, echoing what he had said earlier to Michael.

'How do you know I haven't?' Tom turned around, glaring at him.

'She needs a solicitor, preferably a woman, she needs somebody on her side.'

'How could she have somebody more on her side than you?'

Sam had to acknowledge the justice of this. He and Jess had been friends for years. He would have done anything for her. She was an ideal. She was a pitman's daughter, had no education, few advantages. All she had were her looks, her elegance and her sweet smile.

'She still needs–'

'All right, all right.' Tom put up both

hands in submission. 'I'll talk to her, OK? Just don't sit there and think you know everything.' Tom collapsed back into the chair. 'Will you act for me?'

'I'd rather not.'

'But you will, won't you?' Tom said.

Sam didn't stop for lunch. When Tom had gone his appetite had disappeared. Kathleen brought him a sandwich when she came back from her lunch hour but he didn't eat it and she made him some more coffee and he worked. By half past five he was more than ready to go home but he still had a great deal to do. It was often easier working in the evenings when the others had gone and there were no interruptions but he was not even allowed that. There was a tentative knocking on the thick oak door of his office and Andrew Elliot, the youngest member of the practice, put his head round the door.

'You busy?' Andrew's mother had just died, he had already asked for time off to go to London for the funeral, so Sam could only hope that this was to be something positive.

Andrew Elliot was one of the least competent people he had ever employed. He looked like a boy even though he was twenty-seven and he acted rather like one most of the time. He had been Gareth's choice and for all the wrong reasons.

'His father is Matthew Elliot. We cannot afford to offend him,' Gareth had said.

'So, we have to take his son on?'

'He's our top client. He doesn't have to, he could use other people in London. He's stayed loyal because we are his original solicitors.'

Gareth handled all the work Matthew Elliot sent their way.

'I'd rather do without people like that.'

'We cannot afford to do without him. And why should we? He's a controversial figure. He's well known, rich–'

'He's a ruthless bastard,' Sam said.

'You'd be a ruthless bastard if you'd come up that far–'

'Spare me the details,' Sam said.

'The point is that Andrew is as unlike his father as anybody could be. He's sensitive, nice and he will be an asset to the practice. Old ladies will flock to him. He's just what we need.'

God save me from sensitivity, Sam thought as Andrew closed the office door. Sam had met Matthew Elliot on a good number of occasions and cordially loathed him. He owned restaurants, fashionable high-class furniture shops, carpet warehouses, a clothing chain and probably a great many other things. When he walked into a room every man in the place felt stupid and every woman was ready to drop her knickers, that was what money and power did. Matthew didn't bother to hide behind niceness. When he was in contact over the telephone, the few times Sam had had to deal with him, he was short to the point of brusqueness, but mostly he didn't deal with the practice personally, he got other people to do everything.

Andrew openly hated his father and only saw him when he had to, but he had needed time off lately to see his mother. He waited now to be asked to sit down. He looked nervous.

'I – I need a rise,' he said.

There was something endearing about him, like a teddy bear. Sam was only eight years older but he felt a lot more. His father had always said that intelligence was the greatest luxury of all, so proud of his clever son. Sam felt a slight physical pain when he thought of either of his parents. His father had died of a heart attack when Sam was twenty-seven. His mother had died of lung cancer when he was thirty-four. He had, however, many good memories of a happy and secure childhood, and the knowledge that his parents and his brother had loved him.

As far as Sam could judge, Andrew had been neglected and ignored by his father and pampered by his mother.

'I'm going to ask Alex to marry me,' he said.

Alex Chamberlain was Andrew's answer to his father, the one brilliant spark in his whole life. Sam was amused and rather pleased by it. The first time he had met them he could not think what she had seen in Andrew. She was small, dark, with a gorgeous figure, sweet-faced and clever. She was marketing director for an American company which had factories in the north-east. She was successful, well paid and ten years older than Andrew. Surprisingly, Sam thought, Andrew read his mind.

'I want to do things my way. I want to have enough so that I don't have to rely on Alex. I'd like a family.'

Andrew was due a pay rise but Sam thought he would have given it to him anyway, for such spirit. He didn't see Alex Chamberlain as the kind of woman to stay at home producing children but you could only ever be sure of one thing with people, as far as his experience had taught him – they would always surprise you. It was so nice to have a positive thing happen that Sam smiled.

'It's overdue,' he said and Andrew smiled back at him.

Andrew left at six and Gareth shortly afterwards. Sam waited until about half past seven, the time he judged that Stephen West would be back from work but before he sat down to supper, and then he telephoned. They had not kept in close touch over the years but from time to time he rang to let Stephen know how his parents were. This time Sam chatted uneasily but Stephen saw through it and in the first long pause he said, 'It's my father, isn't it? My mother never tells me anything. You think I should come home?'

Sam made vague noises. He didn't want this to be his decision but neither did he think Stephen should be left unaware that his father was so very ill. Stephen thanked him and said he would sort things out.

Sam worked until almost half past eight and then drove his battered Land Rover out of the town and a few miles into the country.

His house lay on the moors between Allendale Town and Hexham and it was a very special place, a fortified fourteenth-century farmhouse with what one guidebook to the area called 'later additions', not later than the nineteenth century.

Sam and Dominic had been born at the house in Hexham, but they had spent most of their lives here in this house on Hexhamshire Common. As Sam reached it now the moon had risen in a clear cold sky and the outline of the ruins of the building showed up clearly and the more comfortable part of it where he lived was lit and would be warm and cosy. Pam, who did his housekeeping, was a vicar's wife. When he had first met her he couldn't believe she was married to a religious man. She was funny, down to earth and ordinary and she liked coming to his house and keeping order because she said it got her out of the way. She came over for part of each day and he understood why. It wasn't far but it kept her from the telephone and the incessant demands of the parish.

She had no set hours, any time during the day would do and because of her his house was always clean and tidy and neat, with fresh flowers and lovely meals. She was a good cook. Sometimes she baked bread and brought it with her or baked while she was there and he would come back to the smell. She shopped lavishly for him at Marks and Spencer's when she went into Newcastle and he knew that she got a kick out of spending his money freely, because she didn't have much herself.

Otherwise she went mad at the super-market and he would come home to bowls of exotic fruit and champagne vinegar and the expensive olive oil which she knew he liked. Sometimes she and her husband invited Sam over for dinner, from a sense of duty, he thought, and they had been to the farm for tea, but he knew that she liked best coming and being there alone with the radio switched to Radio Two and nobody to disturb her.

She had left the fire banked down in the sitting room but Sam soon brought that back to visible life. There was a casserole at the side of the Rayburn in the kitchen. He slid that on to the heat. He turned on the radio and heard the wistful sound of Satie. He poured himself a glass of wine and sat down.

Friends had expressed astonishment that he did not move after Dominic died. They called the place too big. It had half a dozen bedrooms and all the rooms were large. There were outbuildings, byres and barns and Sam owned a hundred acres, which was let to local farmers. He wouldn't move from here. He knew that people were aware of his prosperity. Women eyed him warmly but Sam never wanted to be close to anyone again in his life.

He sat in front of the fire and ate his supper and then he went outside to look at the stars. It was a frosty night, one of few so far that winter, and up there on the common, where there was nearly always a stiff breeze and sometimes a howling gale, it was completely still. It was such a relief to come back here after the problems of the day. There was nothing to spoil the stars, no light pollution, no noise. People claimed that the house was haunted but Sam knew all the ghosts in his life. He went to bed and slept well.

Two

When Jess had first gone to Germany with her husband she had expected the climate to be better than it was in England, she couldn't think why. They had been there for four years and she had learned German. She wasn't fluent but spoke it sufficiently well so that she insulted no one. Tom had been amused at her efforts. A lot of English and Americans who lived there spoke nothing but their own language. Jess had discovered that the women who served on the delicatessen counter at her local supermarket across the road from her house spoke English, French, Turkish and German, so it seemed the least she could do to address them in their own language.

She was completely happy there. Her life was a fairytale. She had been working in a clothing factory in Hexham when she met Tom in a Newcastle nightclub. She could not believe that somebody like him could love somebody like her.

Her parents had been so proud when she

married him but sorry when they realized she would be going straight to Germany. They missed her. This autumn they had been persuaded to travel to stay with her. There had been direct flights from Newcastle, which made life easier. They stayed for ten days and she enjoyed showing them around, cruising on a big boat down the river, drinking apple wine, eating sausages and exclaiming over the cathedral, the Römerberg – Frankfurt's market square and the Römerhallen, the houses where the gold and silversmiths had lived. They walked in the parks, went to the zoo, and her mother liked the shops.

Her mother had been impressed with the two-storey house within the complex where they lived. Tom had taken her father out to drink beer. He seemed pleased to have them there and she was glad because lately he had been distracted with work, away a lot, not talking much, and she had redoubled her efforts to make their home comfortable and welcoming. There was always good food and wine, she was always there, dressed for him, waiting.

As they cruised down the river she glanced across the table at her father and he smiled admiringly and said, 'Nearly as good as the Tyne.'

Her mother clicked her tongue and raised her eyes. Jess lifted her glass of wine to her lips and Tom got her father to go to the side of the boat to see some important sight.

'I wish you lived a bit nearer,' her mother said.

Jess didn't like to tell her that Tom had been headhunted by a German company which operated in the mid-west of America, and the chances were that within six months he and Jess would be in Springfield, Illinois. He was very good at his job and he was ambitious. He was marketing director, earned a huge salary and was only in his mid-thirties, just the right age to succeed brilliantly. He was so clever and she was so proud of him. He was older than her by eleven years but Jess didn't care about that. When she thought of the men some of her workmates had settled for, Jess couldn't bear to think of it, but she had Tom and they had a future and the pale autumn sunshine and the cool October day, and her mother and father were there and things couldn't get any better.

Later that afternoon when they went home Tom promised to make supper. Their house was upside-down in that the whole of the upper storey was an enormous living room with floor-to-ceiling windows which looked out across the roofs of the city, since they were six storeys high. Tom made chicken and rice, it was the only thing he could do, and they sat there and watched the lights of the city.

When they went to bed she got in beside him and whispered in the darkness, 'When are we going to have a baby?'

'There's plenty of time.'

'I want one now. Let's make a baby, Tom. It could be born next summer.'

'I thought you said the doctor advised waiting three months after you stopped taking the pill. It's been two weeks.'

'Let's do it now, Tom, I want a baby so very much.'

'We'll do it properly when we should. Be patient. We have plenty of time.'

'Let's practise.'

'Not tonight. I'm worn out.'

He turned away from her. Jess lay and watched his back in the varying shadows. It wasn't so very long to wait. She tried to imagine what it would be like the following summer with the baby in the mid-west. They would have a pretty house. Her parents had never been to America. They could come for a long stay. She knew that her mother would be upset, it was such a long way off, so many thousands of miles, but if they had a big enough house, one of those like you saw on television, where the downstairs was all one room and there were lawns around, her mother would like it.

Her own home was a terraced house, two up and two down, with a yard out the back. Her parents had done the best they could, they had knocked through the rooms on the ground floor and it had a new if narrow kitchen and a bathroom on the end of that. The front of the house had a view of the viaduct and the steep-sided valley, but Jess could not believe that she had lived her whole life in such a place before she married Tom. She wondered whether her mother envied her. Her parents seemed happy enough though her father grumbled about work. They wouldn't let her know even if they did have problems, it was not their way. They would come to America and she would take them all over and show them around. She would have one of those big station wagons and they would have barbecues in the back yard. They would like that. In the meanwhile there was Christmas to look forward to. Tom was back and forwards all the time but he had promised that they would go home to Northumberland for the celebrations.

Three

Michael McIver drove his mother-in-law's little Subaru to the side of the road and on to the pavement. There was no garage and not enough room to park a car beside the house. Her home was a forties semi-detached bay-windowed house and, in those days, he thought, there hadn't been the problem of so many cars and nowhere to park them.

The front garden was small and rather overgrown, with a garden shed to one side. The gate wasn't fastened, because the latch was broken, and the door and the bay window needed painting. He had suggested often to Caroline's mother over the years that he would pay for these things but she wouldn't hear of it. Nor did she have enough money to have it done herself. Michael would have been proud to help but to her he was still the boy from Burnside and she would accept nothing from him.

He locked the car and went into the house and shouted that he was home. Soon it would be the only home they had. The company had agreed that he could have six months to leave the house which they had given him in Frankfurt, and that time was almost up.

There was nobody in downstairs. Caroline's mother was the kind of woman who belonged to clubs and was out most days at the church or at various meetings or on arranged outings to the coast or the hills. She had many friends. Michael was fond of her, though it hadn't always been so, she had been disappointed when Caroline married him. He had sworn to show her how well he could do, and he had done, and he would get this job. He had already had two interviews, they were down to the last three people. He had to get it, the money was running out fast. He had spent it on jewellery for Caroline, he had had the school fees to pay at Victoria's exclusive school, which the company had paid up to then, they had been on holiday to the Caribbean, there had been weekends in top-class hotels, good food and wine and new clothes for Caroline, the sort that she deserved.

She came downstairs, kissed him and did a twirl in the hall. It was a new dress in a sort of no-colour like pale sludge, but with her colouring it looked great. They were going to a friend's birthday party that night. He adored her. They had been married for almost twenty years and he considered in that time she had become more beautiful. He loved to think that the clothes she wore were expensive and that he had paid for them. He liked keeping her, telling people that she was his wife. He hated the term 'partner'. It was for people who feared the future, for those who did not take risks, who had no faith in life. Also it sounded like a firm of solicitors, like Browne and Forester, he thought.

Since he and Caroline had been married, Caroline had not worked much until the recent years, when Victoria went away to school and she had little to do, and then she had learned computer skills and gone back to the secretarial work she had done for a couple of years after they were married. He hadn't stopped her, he was not the sort of man who wanted her waiting at home for him out of pride. She had enjoyed having her own money even though they did not need it, but since they had been in Germany she had not worked, and if he was honest he would say that he preferred it but he knew that was selfishness, he wanted to be the centre of her universe.

'I met Sam Browne.'

'Mother says he never goes anywhere or sees anybody. We must invite him at Christmas.'

'I doubt he'll come.'

'He must be lonely, and after what happened to his brother…' Caroline didn't finish the sentence.

'We're going to have the best Christmas ever,' Michael promised her.

'We must do some shopping. It's good of them to let you have this time here, considering we're here for Christmas too. I did so want to be here. How many days will you be in London?'

'Just two,' he said and kissed her.

He wished personally that they had still been in Frankfurt. Christmases there had been wonderful; dances, parties, lots of friends. He missed his friends and he missed the job which he had enjoyed so much and he wished they did not have to stay in the back room of Caroline's mother's house. The bed was uncomfortable and the house they had had in Frankfurt was in a busy area with lots of things happening.

It was too quiet here and he felt the lack of status. They did have friends who they had kept from before he worked abroad, and he knew for all she said that Caroline would have preferred to be in Germany. She liked her mother well enough but living with her was difficult. He thought it must always be so with parents. They had different ideas and his mother-in-law's ideas of how to keep house were not like Caroline's. It was dusty and neglected and she would not let Caroline touch it.

Things would improve. Better times were coming. They would drive to Cumbria to pick up Victoria from school and they would all be together when he came back from London. He had missed her. If he got this job, she wouldn't have to go to boarding school any more, he knew she didn't really like it, even though she didn't say so. This job was based in England. They would have to live near London but Caroline's mother could come and stay, it wasn't far and they would be able to come back here often. He would get the job, he knew that he would.

Four

It was early morning in North London. High above the rooftops, Alex Chamberlain stood naked at the floor-to-ceiling window of the hotel, which looked out over the green of Regent's Park. She had watched the dawn displace the night. She almost bit on the cigarette until she could feel the nicotine coursing its way through her body and calming her. She was so high up, so many storeys above most of London, that her nakedness didn't matter. The windows of the hotel were huge and had – could you call them curtains? – drapes, they were certainly drapes, draped all over the place, great swathes of material, but she felt that they hid her, she liked them.

Beyond, she could see houses, the park and a good many other things which she couldn't identify. From the bed came the soft even breath of sleep. She glanced towards Tom Beardsley and smiled to herself. He was her secret, her adventure, he was fun. Nobody knew and that was the most important thing about it.

She turned back to the window and he stirred and awoke. There were pigeons on the roof opposite, strutting about almost self-consciously, and she thought, though she could not hear the cooing noise they made, they looked so funny and so comfortable. The colours on them were perfect and subtle. No person had ever looked that neat, little ties at the necks, all those lovely iridescent colours in shades of mauve, grey and white.

'Will you come back to Newcastle with me tonight?' said the voice from the bed.

'No.' Alex finished her cigarette and ground it into the small china ashtray on the table by the window.

'Why not?'

'The chances are that Andrew will be travelling back this evening and he thinks I'm in New York. It would look very silly if there I was, large as life, when he got home.'

He came to her and Alex was aware of his body, it was a very good body. She liked him. She didn't love him. He was looking patiently at her, she knew, even though she wasn't turned towards him.

'You're not even married to him,' Tom said.

'I love him.'

'If you loved him you'd be with him today. His mother has just died, for Christ's sake.'

Alex wanted to tell him, because she knew he thought her callous, that she could not bear funerals. The last one she had attended, she had passed out, and that had been very embarrassing. Andrew understood, he didn't even want her there. She would go back to him tomorrow or the next day and she would look after him.

'Why don't you go and shower? You're going to be late,' she said.

Still he hesitated.

'I've been offered the job in Illinois. I want you to come with me.'

'You know very well I can't do that.'

'It's only for a couple of years.'

'Your appointment is in an hour, Tom. Considering the traffic...'

'I want you to think about it,' he said, as he hurried away to the bathroom.

She was alone again, enjoying the best part of the day. She had ordered breakfast earlier and when it arrived was glad she had done so because she was hungry. There was fresh orange juice and hot coffee, croissants and strawberry jam and butter. She felt like a bricklayer with a trowel as she loaded a

42

croissant with jam and butter, watched the butter melt through the hot pastry and, alternating with mouthfuls of coffee, demolished the croissant greedily.

She felt again pangs of guilt that she had not been with Andrew that day. The fact that she had not liked his mother was no excuse. Margaret Elliot had been the kind of woman who didn't drive, didn't drink, didn't go out alone at night, rarely accompanied her husband anywhere.

The first time she had met Andrew's parents his mother had shown her dislike clearly, and why should she not, a little faded middle-aged woman wearing too much jewellery, as though to demonstrate she had it, and expensive clothes which did not show to advantage. It was as if his mother was old, she was like somebody from a previous generation, the kind of person who thought that the smell of warm ironing was halfway to heaven. Alex had friends Margaret's age who were in industry, independent, full of enthusiasm, energy and ideas. Perhaps it was being married to Matthew Elliot all those years that had sapped Margaret's will.

The funny thing was, Alex thought, that the things she despised most about his mother were the things she loved about

Andrew; his gardening, his cooking, the way that he had become a solicitor because he wanted to help people. He must be the only person ever to do so, she thought, most lawyers were in it for the money. Andrew made little money in the country practice where he worked. She loved his naivety, his industry, his enthusiasm for all the divorce cases, the traffic accidents, the wills, the cleaning up after death, the exchange of house contracts.

His mother had been horrified when Andrew announced that he and Alex would live together. Alex's friends had been prophesying for years that she would leave him but she had no intention of doing so. He was the perfect partner. They were so different. He would in time make a good husband, but perhaps not yet, though she thought he had been working up to that lately and she would certainly like to have a child while there was still time.

He was totally dependable, loyal, organized, he took care of everything to do with the house, he kept the accounts and paid the bills and did the shopping. He instructed the cleaner, put away the ironing and, best of all, he was always there for her to come home to. She adored going home to him. He loved their pretentious house and she supposed she loved it too. She could come home to the smell of good food, knowing that the champagne was in the fridge, everything was taken care of and he was waiting. And he was good in bed, it was not that she lacked that. She felt safe with him. She had heard it said that there was only room for one show-off in each family and she was theirs.

Tom, rather like Andrew's father, Matthew, was a self-absorbed bastard, obsessed with his work, and she was never going to go away with him, but she couldn't make him understand. Tom was fun and sometimes exciting. She didn't understand what he was doing with her. Jess Beardsley was beautiful and young and the kind of woman who waited at home for him and it was a much more comfortable arrangement than marriage to herself would have been. However, she thought, Jess had nothing to worry about. He was fun and that was all. He was singing out of tune as he showered.

'Breakfast, Tom!' she shouted.

He came out of the bathroom half-dressed and speedily put on shirt, suit and shoes, slurping down half a cup of coffee. Alex wandered over and kissed him. He put down the coffee and slid both arms around her.

'I went to see my solicitor when I was in Newcastle. I'm getting a divorce. I want you to marry me.'

Alex stood back and frowned.

'You aren't supposed to be with a loser like Andrew,' Tom said, 'and I love you.'

'Tom—'

'Think about it over the weekend. I'm going back to the States and I'm going to take you with me.' And he was gone and she was left, staring at the door.

Five

Stephen and Susan West arrived in Hexham in the snow. They had not been north for five years and then only briefly. His parents had been to London to visit a couple of times a year and it had been enough. His mother had not pretended to get on with Susan and his father hated the city. Before that he had come back only when he had to. In fact he had regarded Northumberland then rather as he regarded London now. When he had been young, he left home to go to Oxford and, after that, London had seemed exciting. It was to do with age, Stephen thought, and he was happy to come home now, at least he would have been had his father been well.

They drove. He was surprised at the short time it took, it had always seemed so far away in his mind, like another world, or was it that he had denied to himself that he could have been back in a morning, had he wished to do so. To him they passed many familiar landmarks but none of it meant anything to

Susan. She came from Hampshire and the move north had not been her idea.

As he drew nearer he drove faster, as though, if he did not keep up, something important would escape. His work had taken him to New York and then back to London and it was glamorous, at least to other people and his wife, forward-thinking, important. It made him laugh to think of it, the right address, the right friends, the best restaurants, the clothes, the cars, the connections.

He had become tired of it. Susan had not wanted children and in some way he felt as though he was going round and round and getting nowhere. She wanted to be free, she said, though free to do what, he had not discovered. She came from Lymington, a prosperous, elegant, exciting place, much warmer than here. Even in summer on the Tyne, it was sometimes cold, and the roses in the little front gardens bloomed long and well through all the rain. The moors were vast and bleak in rain and wind and snow and today were shrouded in mist.

He had woken up one morning and realized that he was bored, not just tired or frustrated because things had gone wrong at work, but screamingly horribly bored by the transient nature of what he did. Little of it seemed to matter other than hard news and even that went round in circles.

'You're a dinosaur, Steve,' his boss, Oliver, had complained when Stephen said that he was leaving. 'What are you going to do, act like some bloody woman who can't cope with a career and kids? Downsizing, is it? Knitting, crafts in the dales? Going to raise your own celery? I'll tell you one thing, Susan will hate it.'

It seemed as if he was finished with that life, because even as he was handing in his notice with no idea of what to do next, and quarrelling with Susan because she had no job and couldn't understand what he was doing, Sam telephoned. They had known one another all their lives, so he was used to the way Sam went on and, through Sam's vague noises about how everything was all right but wasn't it a long time since Stephen had been home, Stephen got the message and then he felt guilty. His father must be much worse, for Sam to telephone like that.

'I have to go, maybe even help out at the pit for a while.'

'You don't know anything about it,' Susan pointed out, horrified.

This wasn't true, he had been brought up

with it, he knew a great deal.

'I'm not going to try and run it,' he said. 'There is a manager. I just want to go and see how my father is and how my mother is managing. We don't have to stay. A few days will make no difference. I need time to think what to do next.'

His mother was relieved rather than pleased to see them, he thought, even though she hugged Susan. He had not known that the house was so run down. How could he have brought her here, he thought? She was a city girl, she loved London. How could he have thought so little of his parents that he did not help them before now, considering how much they needed him? His mother, he thought, had kept a great deal from him. His parents had always seemed able to do everything.

His father was confined to bed and had lost a great deal of weight. Stephen kept a smile on his face that first evening, as he saw how bad his father was, but the shock was hard. When his father was tired Stephen made his way down the big dog-leg staircase, slowly, because he had to face his mother and Susan in the sitting room, he wished in a cowardly way that he had not come back. He had no excuse to stay in

London, nothing to hold him, not even the desire to be there and do the work he was trained for. As he opened the door to the welcome of a big fire and the satisfaction of seeing his mother's pleasure in his presence, he was flooded with gladness that he had come home. He was an only child, there was nobody else to help.

'I'll go and have a look round tomorrow, talk to Langstaff.'

'Mr Langstaff isn't there any longer,' his mother said stiffly. 'Your father wasn't happy with him.'

'So who is running the pit?'

'He was there until last Friday.'

The implication was obvious but Stephen couldn't help being surprised.

'Langstaff is a trained manager. I can't take over from him.'

'Nobody is suggesting that you should. The men know what they are doing and your father has been able to go most days.'

This was so patently not true that Stephen almost said something, his mother's voice rang in the air like off-key notes. How long had she been pretending to herself that his father would get better? How many days had gone past since anybody with authority had gone to the mine?

The night was cold and reminded Stephen of his childhood, freezing bedrooms, chilblains, heavy covers on the bed, not wanting to get up in the mornings or leave the comfort of the living room even as far as the hall. There was linoleum on the floor in their bedroom and only a clippie mat by the bed for your bare feet.

'I remember why I left,' he grumbled as he climbed into bed.

Regardless of the temperature, Susan was wearing the kind of nightdress she specialized in, silky, transparent. She liked sex, they had always been good in bed together. Until lately everything had been good. Somehow when they made love now, it seemed pointless. He couldn't understand that, except that he had seen other people with children.

Making love for pleasure had always been enough in the past, why wasn't it any more? He was no longer so involved. It was almost like being somebody watching, rather embarrassed. It was like an appetite which had to be appeased, another chore, an ordinary mealtime, though there was nothing ordinary about their sex life. She was willing, she was fun and she was clean-limbed and soft. Her breasts had not suckled a child, they

52

were the breasts of a young girl, her thighs had not felt between them a new life.

It had not mattered before. He had liked having her to himself, that and his work and their wonderful lifestyle had been enough. He had cared about food and wine and furniture and holidays and lying in bed late on Sundays and wearing expensive clothes and driving a costly car and suddenly it was empty, stupid, and so was this, he thought, as his wife took in her breath. He could see pleasure in her eyes.

From somewhere outside, owls were calling to one another in the garden. When he had been little his father had named the owls 'Wol A' and 'Wol B', his father who had always been so capable, the provider, the person who locked the doors, walked the dog late beyond the garden walls, knew about politics and money and the ways of the world, which had all been secret to Stephen.

He knew in his heart that something had died in his father when he left. Not that the old man had tried to stop him, he had told Stephen how proud of him he was, how there was nothing in the north and every-thing in London.

Stephen wondered why he had not seen that his parents did not have much money, that his father had struggled with the business for years. He had said not one word. Stephen knew the theory behind it, that the son could not be the father, that children were on loan, that you could not take your child back into your own world, that you must let it go forward into its own, and he wondered how he had become so over-educated, so uncaring, and he wished more than anything in his life that he could have a son.

How predictable, he thought, smiling at himself. Your father's dying and biology must have its way. It was a physical need, this urge for children, he could see them, a little girl holding his hand trustingly as he had held his father's hand, a boy climbing the big trees in the garden and coming home with scabby hands and knees and a dirty face. Children were the only thing that could break your heart, but what else was there? He thought that his father would not live long enough to see a child, even if Susan conceived tonight, and there was no chance of that. She was not interested in children. His parents would have been so pleased. How could he not have seen it?

Susan made quite a bit of noise when they did this, at least when she was having a really good time, which hadn't been often of late. He had pleaded tiredness, work, late meetings, waiting until she was asleep before he came home, and when he had come home she accused him of not paying attention.

The walls of the old house were thick, which made him feel better. He did not want to think of his mother lying alone as she did because his father had a bedroom to himself, they said they were more comfortable that way but he knew that his parents must have done this thousands of times and that his mother was in a cold bed with her thoughts and a dying man next door.

He would have spared her his wife in ecstasy except that it was probably sheer hunger on Susan's part, considering that he had refused her so often lately; it was not expertise or charm, it was bloody neglect that made her cling and whimper. Her whimpers turned to cries, her body was satin with sweat and still he could hear the owls in the garden, above and beyond the noise that she made.

Owls always sounded as though they were almost laughing, he thought, friendly nudging up in the trees, one in the lilac tree beside the far wall and the other probably in the big fir tree which had provided a house or a hiding place or a store depending on what childhood game was in progress. She cried.

'What?' he said.

She shook her head.

'Nothing,' she said.

'Did you hear the owls?'

'Did I what?' She looked at him from the white pillow. Her hair was all over the place. She closed her eyes. She hadn't heard the owls, she didn't hear anything.

Six

After the funeral, when everyone had gone, Andrew didn't know what to say to his father. It was nothing new, he had never known what to say to him, but his mother had always been there between them to fill the silence and now she wasn't.

The caterers were quietly clearing the kitchen of glasses, bottles, plates of finger food. He wished that he could have thought of some excuse to help, but his father had paid for this, just as he paid for everything, and Andrew knew that he should go through into the drawing room and talk. His father had been polite all day. In fact Matthew had been polite all of Andrew's life. Andrew's throat dried as he paused in the doorway of the room; it was fussy, over-furnished, his mother's choice. Andrew knew that his father would have chosen bareness, severity, emptiness – they had not even that in common.

He had seen the way that his father worked, his offices, his restaurants, the word minimalistic could have been in-

vented for them. He could never understand why, over the years, the public had
bought his father's ideas. His father was
always first and people followed. But this
room, as all the rooms in the house, had
been as his mother had chosen and his
father had allowed it to be.

Matthew was standing looking out over
the square. There was no view, not to
Andrew, just more houses, the pavement,
cars. Andrew had left snow in Tynedale but
the grass inside the railings here in north-
west London was wet with rain. He thought
longingly of home.

His father heard him and turned. Andrew's
throat dried even more. In twenty-seven
years his father had not struck him, contra-
dicted him or even raised his voice, yet
Andrew was afraid of him. He feared the
tremendous ability which Matthew had.
Without advantages or education his father
was a brilliant businessman and a multi-mil-
lionaire. Matthew Elliot wore very expensive
clothes. Andrew had no idea how much
money his father spent on things like suits
and shirts and shoes, but even he knew that
some people lived comfortably on less,
because there was absolutely nothing about
them. He was like a bird, a magpie, perfectly

turned out always, his clothes were like an extra skin and he wore them easily as though he had never seen a pit row.

Sometimes he wore dark-grey and it was the only variation, except in summer, when he might venture as far as pale cream, as though colour was just too vulgar for him to consider, or perhaps he didn't consider it, he let his tailor take care of that. He had not, as far as Andrew remembered, ever put on an ounce of weight – he ate sparingly and drank nothing – and he was tall, taller than most men of his generation, he topped six feet by a couple of inches at least and it vexed Andrew that Matthew was bigger than him, it was the wrong way round, that his father should look down on him.

There were no lines of worry on his face, his grey hair was worn very short. He had cold piercing blue eyes and apart from a slight northern accent there was nothing of the miner's son left. He owned this Georgian house, another in New Hampshire with a lake, a house in Majorca with a yacht, and a cottage in Northumberland with a view of Coquet Island. Andrew did not know that his father went to any of the other houses. Matthew didn't tell him anything. They had little contact.

'So,' Matthew said, 'you're going back tonight.'

'Alex is coming home.'

It was a lie but the idea of spending the night here in his father's house was unbearable. Andrew had a woman to go to, a woman as good, no, better than any of the hordes of women his father had ever had, and she loved him. It was one of the mysteries and delights of his life that Alex loved him and that she disliked his father. She didn't hate Matthew, that in itself would have been suspect, she had not even murmured that she didn't like him, but Andrew was cosy with the knowledge. He wished his father loneliness, he wished him grief. He wished that Matthew would shed a single tear over the woman he had been married to for almost thirty years. He wished that he would at least smoke a cigarette or pour generously from a whisky bottle. He had had half a glass of orange juice that day, as far as Andrew was aware.

He thought of his gentle mother. He remembered her best listening to Radio Three and dancing, swaying softly in the kitchen. She was gone from this house and there was no reason for him to stay. A sudden anger engulfed him.

'You didn't love her!' he accused.

Matthew was too clever to argue, Andrew thought bitterly, or to justify himself. He wished the words back. Where had they come from? He had not meant to say anything.

'I'm going home.'

'I'll get Oswald to drive you to the station.'

'Don't bother. I expect never to come here again. I expect and hope never to see you again.'

He walked out, found a cab. When he had left the square, faced the retreating sun beyond the shops in the streets nearby, watched out of the window as they went past Regent's Park, he sat back in the seat and all he felt was relief. He would not have to speak to his father ever again. All those years he had tolerated Matthew out of loyalty to his mother. It was over. He thought of Alex. She was coming home tomorrow, they would be together.

In his mind's eye he could see their house. It was only a few years old, within a walled complex just beyond Hexham. He and Alex had bought it when he joined the country practice. There was a swimming pool, a health club with a jacuzzi, sauna and steam room, and there were squash courts and tennis courts and a security system with a caretaker. Alex had a good salary so they paid their mortgage easily. She drove a Jaguar and wore designer clothes. They had lots of parties, mostly for her friends. They called him 'Alex's toy boy' behind his back.

Andrew always asked Sam and Gareth, the partners from the practice, to the parties. Gareth looked like a California beach boy, women couldn't resist him, tall, blond and frivolous. He usually brought a woman who wasn't his wife and almost always got drunk.

Sam always refused. Sam's refusals made Andrew feel as though he and Alex and their friends weren't good enough for him. How different the two men were, Gareth handsome, brash and open, Sam quiet, shabby-suited and efficient, and it irked Andrew to think that Sam Browne apparently despised him and his beautiful partner and their fashionable and successful friends and their new home.

As far as Andrew could judge, all Sam had was his work. He was very good, his reputation throughout the area was sound and many people had told Andrew so. Once, sitting in the passenger seat of Sam's battered Land Rover, he had ventured, 'You never come to our parties. What do you do at weekends?'

Sam shrugged and was vague. They had never been invited to his house either; nobody, as far as Andrew could tell, ever was. And he had been past it and thought that it looked like a magical place, there was an air about it, a wistful, watching, almost beckoning light, yet people were denied entrance. It was as though invisible warriors surrounded the old building, or a moat. You might be carried off there and never return, go through the gate and vanish into the mists, like Avalon.

Sam ate tuna-fish sandwiches in the office at lunchtime and then went home and, as far as Andrew could discover, that was all. There was no mystery. People said that Sam had been married once but nobody knew anything about it except that it was over. There was no woman. He seemed to have no friends. There was not even any giveaway in his office, no photographs, no books other than essential ones, no expensive leather chair as Gareth had.

There were a couple of ornaments in the office, china birds. They looked to Andrew's untutored eyes as though they were valuable. His father would have known. They sat atop the only decent piece of furniture in the room, an old oak bookcase, beside the

63

window, and the birds were placed as though they were about to fly. They were white, perhaps they were gulls, it was difficult to tell. Apart from that, it was always slightly untidy, as though Sam was too caught up in the problems of his clients to care, and quite often he did work cheaply.

Sometimes, so Gareth had intimated when drunk, Sam would have them work for nothing, for feckless people. Who did he think he was, Gareth had said, waving his glass around in his hand in one large gesture, Robin Hood? Gareth attracted the right kind of clients, and there were plenty of those, but many of Sam's clients were ill-clothed and ill-shod and had thick local accents, old people, snotty children, clothes that reeked of farmyards and second-hand shops, hands that worked hard. It did the practice no good, Gareth said.

In the beginning Andrew had wanted to help Sam, had wanted to admire him, but it was Gareth who treated him as an equal, Gareth he became friendly with. Gareth owned a BMW and lived in a detached house with big gardens on the edge of Hexham. He had parties there, to which Alex and Andrew were always asked. Gareth had a pretty blonde wife and two blonde children. Sam continued to refuse invitations.

It would be Gareth's thirty-fifth birthday soon and there was sure to be a big bash. It would be something to look forward to after Christmas. Christmas itself would be one long party and Alex would be there for a whole week. Andrew smiled as he reached King's Cross. In three or four hours he would be home.

Seven

Michael felt as though he could have run home without the help of the train. He had got the job, a good salary, a new car, moving expenses. They could live near London, not in a good part, but within an hour's train journey, maybe in a new house, and Victoria could go to school nearby, something she had longed to do. He would not even have to tell Caroline that he had been made redundant, just that he had a new job and they could live the lifestyle as he had always sworn they would keep on doing. Everything would be perfect. He had seen Tom Beardsley as they got on. They had worked together in Frankfurt, so they changed seats and sat together and Andrew Elliot, who worked for Sam, was in the same first-class carriage. Michael knew the Elliot family, most of whom lived in the village he came from.

Soon Michael couldn't see much. It was a dark autumn afternoon and rain began to fall across the windows as the train pulled out of the station. It was comfortable. He had always liked travelling by train and here in first class they provided free tea and coffee and would bring drinks and sandwiches to you. He told the other two men his good news and they decided that it called for celebration, so they went off to the dining car and ordered wine and good food.

Michael was happy. Caroline would come to Newcastle to meet the train, she was so eager to see him. He had told her nothing but she would be surprised and pleased. Her mother would be pleased too that he had found a job in this country. Maybe they would be able to find her a little house near to them. Caroline's mother was fiercely independent and, although she had flown to Frankfurt twice while they had been out there, she would be pleased to have them back in England. She had no other ties in Hexham. He would suggest to her that she came to live near them or even that she could sell her house and he would get a big mortgage and with her capital and his earning capacity they could buy a house with a flat so that she could be nearby. Caroline had often worried about leaving her mother alone, even though she had lots of friends and had never suggested to them that she was lonely.

The first part of the journey was quite funny. Lots of commuters caught that train and got off at Stevenage. One man burst into the dining car, snatched up a bottle of wine from the table and ran off the train. To the amusement of the other passengers, two members of the crew chased him up the platform. Tom Beardsley laughed, leaned across the table when they had been stuck there for fifteen minutes and said, 'Let's have a whip round and pay for it or we'll be here all night.'

Michael had tried to say all the right things to Andrew about his mother. Andrew seemed to cheer up a bit after he had had a glass of wine and a plate of chicken with wine and garlic, buttered vegetables and tiny new potatoes.

The train set off again. Michael was enjoying himself but he just wanted to get back and tell Caroline the news. He couldn't wait to see his family. Tom was quite subdued, as though he didn't want to go home. They finished their meal and went off back to their first-class carriage. By that time the train had reached Doncaster. Michael knew that it was a silly idea but when they got to Doncaster he always felt as though he was almost home. From there it was not far to York. From York it was just over an hour to Newcastle.

They settled themselves down again. Michael was completely happy if rather exhausted and full of dinner and a couple of glasses of wine. He listened to the sound of Tom and Andrew talking and their voices got softer and softer until they faded from him altogether.

He awoke to a feeling of tremendous impact and the sound of terrified people screaming in panic. Tom Beardsley, sitting opposite, was covered in blood and everywhere there was glass, the window had smashed, the frame had come out and hit him. Andrew was unconscious on the floor, and then the lights went out. Michael was amazed that he was not hurt. He felt nothing, only the table in front of him, but he could not move, he could not speak, as though he was not there at all. The last sound he heard was the noise of somebody's mobile phone in amongst the screaming.

Eight

Matthew was glad he had gone to work, even though the breakfast meeting was dragging, at least by his standards. He had tried not to think, on the way there, about Margaret or Andrew or anything which mattered. He hadn't slept, he hadn't eaten, time had altered and was going past almost on its own, his mind was full of loss and his fears for the future. Work seemed an unnecessary interruption but he had known that he must go. He had several important meetings that day. He had managed to shower and dress and get out of the house. He wasn't even tired. He sat back in the car on the way to work as Oswald drove, ignored the traffic and the street scenes, gazed out of the window.

He thought of the way Andrew had left the day before. He thought how unsatisfactory that leaving had been. He didn't want to think about the funeral, the silence of the house, how Margaret was dead. He had turned off the phones and gone to bed.

He was grateful now that he had had to come to his office in the middle of the city. Everything went on the same here, it did not matter that people died, that his son had left him alone, that the house was so empty. Here he could work just as he did every day. It was enough to distract him. It was such a relief. But boredom was setting in, people were making obvious remarks, it was all slowing down. Just as his concentration began to slide, his secretary, Kate, came in as though on cue and whispered in his ear, 'There's a telephone call for you.'

He was grateful. Perhaps she knew that he needed rescuing, but then she would not have interrupted him for anything which was not important. He excused himself and followed her along the soundless carpeted corridor to his office, where he picked up the receiver.

'Hello?'

'Matthew, is that you?'

He recognized Alex's voice even though they rarely spoke on the telephone or anywhere else for that matter, even though her voice was rasping and she began to cry, a horrible snotty thick sound.

'Alex?'

'Matthew? I've been trying to get you.

71

Wherever have you been?'

He hadn't seen her in months, she hadn't even bothered to cut short her business trip and support Andrew at his mother's funeral. He didn't answer.

'I'm at the – the Regent's West. Can you come over?'

Matthew didn't say any of the things which went through his brain. She would not ask him there unless something serious had happened.

'Yes, of course,' he said and rang off.

When he got there and took the lift up to the fourteenth floor and knocked on the door, a policewoman opened it and Matthew recognized the smell instantly, it was grief. He had heard it said that people kept away from the widowed because they smelled of the dead but he had not realized that it was so. It made him want to shudder.

Alex was wearing a short dressing gown – if you could have described such a small garment as a dressing gown – and little else as far as he could judge. She had no idea where she was or of the mess of her face, which was blotched red and white, thick lines of mascara, her mouth like blubber and her eyes small with crying. Matthew felt a wave of nausea. The policewoman began to speak but Alex ran to him.

'They think Andrew's dead.'

Matthew looked at the policewoman. She looked back at him as though he should have known, though all she said was, 'The London to Newcastle derailed last night. We think that Mr Elliot was on board.'

To his shame, possibly for the first time in his life, Matthew had avoided the news overnight. He had felt that he could not stand any more. Now he might have to. He would not think about his own feelings. Alex should be his first concern and that was why she had telephoned. She could not cope. It would not do that neither of them could cope. He would keep that in mind.

After a while she was persuaded to put on some clothes because one of them at least must go north to the hospital. She smoked – Matthew had forgotten how awful the smell was. She drank whisky, the fumes were sweet.

'I want to go home. We could go by bus; those awful sandwiches, that appalling coffee and the top of the bus, swaying like a branch.'

He drove. She didn't sleep in the car. She was tired certainly but the shock kept her awake. It was not that far in a fast car and this was a Mercedes. She lay back in the comfortable passenger seat and closed her eyes but she would not sleep for many days to come, he knew.

When the grisly bit at the hospital was done, they went on to the dreadful house which Andrew had been so proud of and to which Matthew had never been invited. The curtains, his critical eye told him, would have graced a theatre, they were so generous and loud. The carpets would have hidden a small cat. The kitchen would have defied a spaceman and the bathroom had huge tiles like the lavatory at Brighton station. The lamps had tassels, the books had bright gold leather bindings, the gardens beyond would have given Hampton Court Palace a run for its money. Matthew didn't see the swimming pool. It was the only good thing about his day.

The evening closed in early. It had been almost dark at three. At five it was pitch black except for the stars and that here there were artificial lights all over the place. It was like Blackpool in October and some people had already bowed to Christmas, because the trees were tiny dots of colour, some of them flashing on and off.

Matthew went outside. The garden next

door had stone lions, at least a dozen of them, placed carefully here and there like giant gnomes. Beyond the houses were huge black gates where only certain people were admitted. It was like hell.

At eight o'clock, but not before the whisky bottle was empty, Alex passed out. Matthew left her there on the sofa and searched the kitchen fruitlessly for decaffeinated coffee. There was only a packet of something called Australian Peaberry. He broke it open, the smell nearly knocked him sideways, it was so sweet and rich brown. He found a cafetière and made far too much. It tasted sludge-like, almost as thick as chocolate. His head spun. He went back into the sitting room with a big mugful and sat down and watched her sleep.

Nine

Jess flew home from Frankfurt. Her father met her at Newcastle and took her back to Burnside Village. It was her worst nightmare. In a way it seemed that she had never left and that the time in between, her marriage to Tom, had been a dream, because fairy tales like that didn't really come true, it was only in love stories where wonderful Mills and Boon men, good-looking, clever and rich, married women like her.

She was no longer beautiful. She had lost half a stone in less than a week and hadn't slept for more than an hour a day. She had thought she would be numb for ever.

The villagers were full of talk about the crash and the way that the goods train which had ploughed into the passenger train had been carrying a thousand tons of imported coal.

Jess went to see their solicitor, Sam Browne. Sam explained everything to her in what Jess thought of as nicely neutral tones. He sat back in the old leather chair.

'You'll be fine for money when things get sorted out,' he said. 'In the meanwhile you have quite a bit of your own.'

Jess stared to the side of him and wondered whether Sam had deliberately chosen an office with the kind of view which gave people an excuse to look away from him. Outside, Tynedale went neatly up in walled fields and there were sheep and trees and snow along the edges of the fields, under walls and on the tops. Beyond the window she could hear the dull sounds of the town, traffic and voices.

Sam was regarding her with care.

'I'm so sorry, Jess.'

Everybody was sorry, so many people had told her that, but somehow it was different when Sam said it, because he had been through so much in his life, you knew that he meant it. Sam had always liked her. She had never thought particularly about it before, men did like her, but this was not a physical thing, at least, it was not just a physical thing, she knew. Sam liked her in a professional capacity, he would look after her legally and he would advise her in all kinds of other ways, she knew that she could rely on him. Sam's office was the only place at present where Jess felt safe. She wished she could have curled up on the floor by the window like a spaniel and stayed there for ever.

'I don't know what to do next.'

'Then don't do anything,' Sam said. 'When you want to, come back and we'll talk and I'll get you the best help, whatever you need.'

There were forms to sign, there were always forms to sign everywhere she went, the dull business of death was complicated. She signed the forms and thanked him and went back to Burnside.

Her parents would have been upset had she not stayed with them and she was sleeping in the same room that was hers before she had left to get married, since there were only two bedrooms. There the terrors nightly fell in on her. Tom was not coming back. But for the money he had left her and his possessions, there would be nothing.

In winter the village always looked bleak but, before, it had been beautiful, the dramatic countryside around it, the farms, the moors, the castles, the steep hillsides, the brown beck which gave the place its name. There had been a Benedictine convent there, which was burned by the Scots late in the thirteenth century. Was that what gave it its unquietness, a meeting between the spiritual and the brutal, which made its way down the centuries?

The little houses clung to the hillside and it was steep, down past the chapel, down past the church with its gravestones, down past the terraces of homes of people whom she knew, the pub, the post office and the shops. If you went far enough you came in time to the bridge over the stream in the bottom, but their terrace was not that far. Chapel Street.

She had been born there and had lived there all her life until she left to get married. She was once again a daughter there. She lay in a single bed with the same furniture which had been in the room since she was a teenager and wept as quietly as she could, because her parents were lying together through the wall.

What right had they, her bitter self was already asking, to be together when she and Tom would not be together again, and, because she loved them, it made her feel worse. Bitterness and envy were difficult to deny, and the increasingly large feeling of having been robbed. The world's biggest burglar had stolen Tom away and nothing would ever bring him back.

Ten

Sam had had to ask where Caroline McIver's mother lived, having discovered that this was where she was staying. When he parked his old Land Rover, his hopes disappeared. If Caroline's mother had had money, this would not have been as difficult, but it was obvious she did not. The street was post-war, it was shabby, run-down, the cars in the street were old ones.

It was early evening. He rang the bell and Caroline answered. She had been a pretty woman but grief had wiped it from her. She was thin, her green eyes were lifeless and so was her hair, which straggled to her narrow hunched shoulders.

There was still, however, something about her which appealed to him. He tried to tell himself it was just professional, he cared for all the people who came to him for legal help, but it was more than that. He had a terrible desire to get hold of Caroline McIver and hug her very close and tell her everything would be all right, when it so obviously would not.

'Mrs McIver, you do remember me? I'm Sam Browne, solicitor.'

She said that she did, though it was obvious to him she remembered nothing, she was in shock. She took him into the hall. An older woman peeped her head around the kitchen door.

'It's Mr Browne, Mother,' Caroline said, 'I'm taking him into the sitting room.'

The woman nodded and went back into the kitchen. The sitting room was small and crammed with furniture, a brown sofa and two well-worn armchairs. A television stood in the corner to one side of the window and in every available space there were tables and ornaments, a china cabinet filled with pink and white crockery and, on the wall, plates and pictures and, on the tables and the cabinet and a dresser, photographs in frames. It was dusty.

Caroline sat him down, offered him tea.

'Did – did my husband make a will?'

'Not that I'm aware of. Do you have a solicitor other than me?'

'No, we always used your firm. I just thought...'

This was getting harder by the second. Her eyes were hopeless, almost colourless.

'There was nothing. I mean, we own nothing.'

'A house?'

'Rented from the company. We always spent everything – holidays, clothes, nice food...'

'Life insurance?'

'No.'

Sam was irritated, firstly at Gareth, who had mostly dealt with Michael and had obviously not advised him well, and at Michael McIver, even though the man was dead. Had he not had enough sense to provide for his family if he should die? He had a wife and a child. Had he no insurance, no savings? Had the man thought he was immortal? Worst of all, Sam had to make a difficult decision now. He should have been used to it, he had to make a great many in his work, but you didn't get used to it.

'I met Michael last week in town and ... you're going to have to forgive me if I'm making a mistake or a very bad error of judgement here. I have to take the chance. He told me that he had lost his job.'

'What?'

'Yes, he – he had an interview last week, it was the third interview, I think. That was why he went to London.'

'There's no money in the account. I couldn't understand it. I was going to sort it out now that – that everything is finished. I didn't know ... there's nothing left.'

'Do you have money of your own?'

'We always had separate bank accounts. All I had was the housekeeping in mine and a little money for what I wanted. Michael liked to buy presents, to give us surprises.'

'A car? Anything you can sell?'

'Nothing.'

'What can you do?'

'I'm a secretary, at least I was.' Her voice had got faint and small. A single tear reached her mouth. She wiped it away with the palm of her hand. 'I worked in a solicitor's office for a while,' she said and smiled.

'What, here?'

'Allgood and Armstrong.'

'Right,' Sam said. 'My partner is looking for a secretary. I'll have a word with him for you.'

Her mother came into the room, cup and saucer in hand.

'Tea, Mr Browne?' she said.

Caroline waited for Sam to go, she needed to take in the fact that for months Michael had had no job and had not told her and she didn't understand why. At least, she did in a way, and it was endearing, but she wished that he could have trusted and confided in her. She wondered whether he had got the new job. If he had, he would have been coming home to tell her. How different it would have been.

Her mother had gone back into the kitchen and Victoria had come downstairs and was talking to her grandmother. She didn't want to face them just yet, to tell them that Michael had deceived them, even though she was sure it had been out of love. Five months ago this would have been a catastrophe, now it was just another blow. After everything that had happened, this almost bounced off her, only the major things mattered any more. Death gave you a sense of perspective.

Later, in the tiny back bedroom where Victoria was sleeping, Caroline told her and added, 'You won't be able to go back to school, we can't afford it.'

'Well, thank God for that,' Victoria said, 'I couldn't stand the place.'

Caroline was astonished.

'I thought you liked it.'

Her daughter looked clearly at her from Michael's soft blue eyes.

'There wasn't much you could do from Germany. I'll get a job.'

'You can go to school here.'

'I've spent quite enough time at school, thank you.'

'But you're in the middle of your "A" levels.'

'You didn't really think I was going to pass them?'

Caroline tried to look ... she wasn't quite sure how. Her daughter was anything but academic. Victoria was practical.

'We'll both have to get a job,' she said.

It was true, Caroline thought, as she trudged down the stairs. She had no house, no car and no money. She did have a lot of unsuitable clothes, the kind you went out to dinner and dancing in, shoes with high heels, sheer stockings, pretty underwear and the kind of nightclothes you wore when you were sleeping with a man. All of that was now unnecessary and most of it was too big, her weight was dropping.

Each day was harder. There was nothing to get up for and her mind would not accept that things were different. She awoke in expectation of being in Germany and of Michael not being dead. She received a telephone call from Sam Browne saying that she could come and see his partner. She tried to dress as she thought a secretary might, and to be confident and unwoolly minded but it wasn't easy.

The receptionist in the hall of the old building asked her to wait and she was kept waiting for almost twenty minutes. There were plenty of seats in a square and magazines which told you all you needed to know about local sheep and cattle sales.

The receptionist eventually led her up wide stairs and along a wider hall and into an office that had modern furniture which she thought looked out of place. She disliked Gareth Forester on sight and it seemed to her that he had been talked into this by Sam Browne, though she couldn't think why. He fired questions at her. She didn't remember afterwards what he had said and when all he said to her was, 'We'll let you know,' she was sure she had failed. Gareth Forester was probably looking for somebody blonde and twenty-three with a good figure.

'Forty?' Gareth had looked hard at Sam.
  'Forty isn't the end of life, you know.'
  'It is for women.'
  'Don't be crass. She's very attractive.'

'Oh God, I hate that.' Gareth got up from behind his desk. 'Go on, tell me she has a winning personality.'

'She has green eyes and red hair.'

'Legs?'

'Two, at least as far as I remember.'

'Funny. Reasonable then.'

'Oh, a lot better than that. Will you see her?'

'Do I have a choice?'

Two days later Caroline had a letter which told her that she had got the job. She could see the relief on her mother's face when she went back with the news. Victoria was frank.

'I've got a job too. At the tea seller's in the marketplace. It's only part-time but when they see how good I am they'll take me on full-time.'

Caroline was glad to see that her daughter was taking the whole thing so well.

It amazed Caroline, the speed at which things altered. Michael had been dead for only three weeks and they had lost everything, but they both had jobs.

She did not enjoy working for Gareth. He made her face burn, the way that he looked at her and, though it should not have mattered, it did, to be looked at like an object,

87

and when she was feeling vulnerable to men for the first time since her marriage almost twenty years ago. He terrified her with his lecherous blue eyes, though he didn't suggest or do anything which could have been seen as offensive. Ivy, who worked as a receptionist, told her not to worry.

'He's harmless,' she said, 'he just thinks he's God's gift.'

That made Caroline smile.

'And isn't he then, Ivy?'

'Give over,' Ivy said.

But his manner made her aware all the time that she was not married any more. It was a hollow feeling, a lonely echoing emptiness which nothing could fill.

Gareth was not fair to her. He got her to buy flowers for his wife and go shopping in her lunch hour, pick up his dry cleaning, run errands, and he got through an astonishing number of clients, so quite often Caroline had to stay late, work she did not get paid for.

She also tried to help with the housework and the washing and ironing. She had not realized that being without Michael would be so tiring, missing him, wanting him, waking up without him, getting through the day without him and, worst of all, going to bed without him. She fell asleep one cold afternoon at her desk and, the next thing she knew, Gareth was bellowing in her ear.

'We don't pay you to sleep!'

Caroline sat up quickly to see him thrust in front of her face a letter which he said had half a dozen typing errors on the first page and three on the second. Without warning, Caroline began to cry. She ran out of the office and towards the ladies' room across the hall. Sam chose that moment to walk into her office and unfortunately Caroline heard the conversation.

'Must you take on strays? She's incompetent. Her husband's been dead a couple of months. What the hell are we doing employing her? We should do like they used to do in India and burn widows, much kinder.'

The tears, which had been running through Caroline's fingers, were stopped by the anger which rose hotly in her head. She didn't make it into the ladies' room. It was the first time she had felt anything but grief for weeks. She didn't give Sam Browne time to reply. She shot back into the room, glaring at Gareth through her tears.

'You bastard!' she said. 'How dare you? You get me cheap. I stay after office hours almost every evening. I put up with you and your bad manners. I'm not here to do your shopping in my lunch hour or send presents to your wife or any of the extra one thousand things you're too sodding idle to do yourself.' She stopped there, her heart was thumping like it would burst through her skin.

'I suppose you think you can walk out of here and find yourself a job somewhere else,' Gareth said, almost shouting back.

'That's enough,' Sam said, and he took her lightly by the arm and led her into his office just in time to prevent her from telling Gareth he could stick his job up his arse.

Sam sat her down in his comfortable chair behind the desk and went back to the door to say into the hall, where Ivy and Kathleen were watching, very interested, 'Make some tea, would you, please?'

Caroline was trembling. She shook so much she didn't think she would ever stop and the tears had begun again, great gulping sobs which it seemed she had kept back for so many days that they had welled there behind the dam and now, with the door shut in Sam's office and the white birds about to fly from their porcelain perch by the window, she could hold back no longer. Sam gave her a box of tissues and busied himself tidying up some papers.

When the tea came she didn't trust herself to pick up a cup and saucer, she just nodded when Sam put them down on the desk in front of her, but even the sound of the teapot pouring was reassuring and the steam rose from the cup and after a while he handed the cup and saucer to her and Caroline wobbled the cup to her lips and took a scalding sip. Sam went on looking at papers and ignored her until she had drunk her tea and by then she had stopped crying and shaking.

'He doesn't mean it, he's just stupid,' Sam said. 'But you're right, he's not entitled to extra time or your lunch hour.' He said other things too, none of which Caroline listened to particularly, and she thought he didn't say anything in particular, he probably knew that the sound of his soft reassuring voice was enough for most people.

Caroline thanked him and went back to her office. Gareth was sitting on her desk, looking contrite, possibly for the first time in his life.

'I'm sorry. I know I'm an idiot but I don't mean it. I can't help being that way.'

She looked at him. Most women would

have admired what they saw. He was almost a perfect specimen, his hair providentially in his eyes, from which the deep blue gaze was like a summer sea. Caroline said nothing.

'My next appointment is at four. You might retype those letters before then,' he said and he went into his office and closed the door.

Eleven

Andrew had left everything to Alex. He had no one else to leave it to. Was this meant to be an excuse, she wondered? She wished that he had not loved her, she wished that she had not loved him, but more than anything in the world she wished that she had not had an affair with Tom Beardsley. Her guilt almost consumed her. Tom and Andrew were both dead. How in hell could any woman lose two lovers in one accident? She should telephone the *Guinness Book of Records*. It could have no equal. Worst of all, she couldn't tell anybody, she went on hour after agonizing hour. She understood the use of a priest, the need for a God, the desire to tell somebody.

Sam Browne was looking sympathetically at her across the desk. She liked his shabby office, his world-weary eyes, but he was not the person she should talk to. They didn't know each other that well. Solicitors dealt with legalities only. They were not friends, he had never come to her parties, he had always avoided her, she knew he didn't like her, even though there was no trace of that here, he was professional.

'I think I might sell the house,' she said briskly.

'Where would you move to?'

'I don't know.' She looked beyond him. She had done too much crying already and she didn't know this man. If he had ever shown himself to be human – if he had been like Gareth and got drunk and gone with other women... She didn't believe Sam had ever drunk too much or had an affair or done anything remotely human. He was too good to live, she thought in exasperation. How could you tell somebody like him? He would never understand. 'Just to get away. Would you deal with that for me?'

'We deal with everything, it's a general country practice.'

'You live alone, don't you? Is it something you get used to?' She made herself look into Sam's eyes.

'Some days I love it. Some days I can't bear it, much the same as any way of living, I think. Do you have family?'

'My father walked out when I was six months old. I can't say that I remember it. My mother died. My only relative, if you can call him that when Andrew and I weren't married, is Matthew Elliot. Do you see how difficult that is?'

'I have to say I can't see him in the role.'

'He's very attentive. He'll probably buy me knitting needles and slippers for my birthday.'

Sam smiled. The smile warmed his eyes and encouraged confidences. Alex looked away and tried to stop herself from saying any more. She got up and went to the window.

'It's one hell of a view,' she said, regarding the fields, the sheep and the fell tops with a shiver.

'Would you be offended if I offered you my opinion?'

'Go ahead.'

'Are you financially straitened?'

'No. No, I'm not.' She wheeled around. His eyes were shrewd yet soft. How did he manage that?

'You can't sell, of course, until probate comes through. Until then, maybe you shouldn't think of selling.'

'Why?'

'No reason. It's just that sometimes when people do things like that quickly they wish they hadn't later.'

'Do you mean memories?'

'Not exactly. You carry those with you, don't you? I'm not sure what I mean, maybe just that you don't need any more pressure.'

'Mr Browne—'

'You can call me Sam.'

'I would if you had ever come to my parties.'

'I'm not much good at parties. I can never think of anything to say.'

'I don't believe you. I made a mistake, you see. It was a very bad one. Did you ever do that?'

'Several times. Why don't you sit down? Ivy makes terrible tea. I'm sure you'd like some.'

'I can't. It isn't a legal matter.'

'Sit down,' Sam said again and smiled and he got up and ordered tea and they waited until it arrived, and there was something about it, the pink and white cups, the big teapot, the shortbread.

'I'm taking up your time.'

'It isn't that precious,' he said.

She couldn't eat the shortbread, even though it smelled warm and sweet and was probably hand-made from some little bakery nearby which made everything in the back room. She wished she had not got this far or that she could run from the room but there was nobody else to talk to.

'I heard it said once that everybody is allowed one very bad mistake,' Sam said.

'You won't tell anybody?'

Sam looked at her.

'Everything said here is confidential.'

'Even personal things?'

'Especially personal things.'

Alex swallowed half a cup of tea and put down her cup and saucer. She looked straight at Sam Browne.

'Tom Beardsley and I were having an affair.'

He tried to disguise the shock on his face and didn't quite manage it for a second or two, and he was surprised too, she could tell.

'It wasn't meant to be important, it was just... Tom was in London a lot and he was fun and ... Americans are so open and charming and he could be gentlemanly. I know it sounds silly but Englishmen don't open car doors for you or let you go first into places. He had plenty of money. We stayed at wonderful hotels and went to fashionable restaurants and we went dancing.' She wiped away tears she had not known were falling and said stupidly, 'Do you go dancing?'

'No.'

'We were often in the same countries or managed to be. We met in New York several times and in Paris. We did silly things, tourist things sometimes and it was never serious ... until just before Tom died. We went to art galleries, we liked the same paintings and the same music and ... I feel so awful, so guilty. Andrew is dead and I was fooling about with Tom.'

'He didn't know,' Sam said.

She couldn't believe he had said it. She smiled.

'I would give up Tom a thousand times to spend another week with Andrew.'

'You can't know what's going to happen and you can't go on blaming yourself. Don't spoil the rest of your life over this. Andrew wouldn't want that.'

Sam wasn't sure if he had known that Alex and Tom had been lovers before she told him or not. Perhaps he had known and dismissed it as too much of a coincidence. Perhaps he had known the minute she walked in the door. She had about her the invisible baggage of the repentant. You could say what you liked about religion, he thought, but people needed priests. The burden of sin was too heavy to be carried. You could argue, of course, that the Church handed people sin as a form of control. Whatever, Alex needed to talk and he could see it.

Both men were dead and if she was to survive she had to overcome that guilt. He knew a lot about survival, it was not really over-the-edge stuff as the inexperienced imagined, it was the ability to get out of bed in the mornings and the kind of far-sighted wisdom which allowed you to lie there when you must. Alex needed to see herself as a person worthy of sympathy.

He gave her tea. He watched her cry. He wished he could keep her safe from any harm. It was not an exclusive wish. The need to protect extended to most of his clients. He felt as though he was there for them to hide behind.

'Tom wanted me to go away with him. Oh God, Sam, I ruined his marriage–'

'That's not the way it works,' Sam cut in. He could see the hope in her face. 'There had to be something wrong with the marriage first.'

'How do you know that?'

'Because it's my job to know it. There is always something wrong. If people had perfect relationships they would have nothing to look outside for.'

'I had a good relationship.'

'You were bored,' Sam said flatly. 'You would have left Andrew eventually. Probably not for Tom but for somebody else. That's the way life is. People shouldn't have to stay with other people because they have no choice. They are entitled to their own lives. You have an obligation to yourself to do what you can to be happy.'

He said more. He preached such litanies to dozens of people. Why could they not be kind to themselves? They had to be given permission to forgive themselves what they would much more easily have forgiven other people. She was skinny and white-faced and anxious-eyed, but when she left she looked better. He was tired though. He hadn't drunk his tea and he hadn't eaten all day. He would go home early and–

Here Kathleen cut in. There was somebody on the telephone. Sam sighed and answered it and made his voice friendly but firm and the tea in the pot grew cold.

Alex went back to work. There she could pretend that Andrew and Tom were both alive. She did not contact Matthew even though he left several messages on her answering machine. She did not give him the

100

number of her mobile phone, she did not want to hear his voice. At first she had kept close to him, he did everything with ease, he was the only person who did not make stupid remarks.

After the first few days, she didn't see him or hear from him. At a distance, it was easy to blame him for what had happened. But for him, Andrew would have been bold, confident, and she would not have gone to Tom. How useful.

She saw him as she passed through London later that month. He was having dinner at a very exclusive restaurant in Westminster. She had gone there with friends and she could see him across the room, with the kind of woman who was so beautiful she could stop traffic. He was not smiling or talking, just sitting listening, and she remembered how good he was at listening. Had he lost his wife and child and cared so little that he could sit calmly there with a tall elegant blonde in a black dress who would undoubtedly take her knickers off for him later?

Alex wanted to go over and throw soup at him. Her rage boiled. She couldn't eat, drink or pay attention to the conversation. She had the horrible feeling that Andrew was at home, waiting for her, or worse still that he knew she had been unfaithful to him again and again with Tom. She hated herself for that. She wondered whether this was the payment, that Andrew had gone from her because she had not valued him sufficiently. She had three glasses of wine, even though they made her feel nauseous, and then to her dismay Matthew saw her and came over.

'Alex. How are you?'

'Never better.'

Matthew looked her over carefully, as though she was a small child and had fallen down and he was checking her for grazed knees. She couldn't introduce him to her friends, she suddenly couldn't remember their names. Matthew said all the right things, it was one of his talents, his soft rich northern voice was like an elastoplast. He asked her where she was staying and when she had told him he said she should keep in touch and he went back to the blonde woman and shortly after that he left.

Alex even managed to eat her dessert, it was a crème caramel concoction. She didn't throw it up until two hours later, alone in her hotel bedroom. From her bed she could hear the sounds of doors opening and closing and of footsteps overhead and muted conversation. She pulled a pillow against her and tried to sleep. The nausea increased. She got up and ran for the bathroom and there it came up, crème caramel, three glasses of wine and some disgusting salad with dressing.

There was a knock on the door and when she had washed her face, gone back into the bedroom and opened the door, it was Matthew. She was astonished. He came in and closed the door.

'Have you considered a holiday?'

'I'm better at work. I just drank too much.'

'You could go to the cottage in Northumberland.'

She looked at him.

'What would I do there?'

'Sleep maybe. You look...'

'Go on, tell me. How do I look? Bereaved, sorrowful–'

'Like you haven't slept or eaten properly.'

Matthew put a small object with a tag down on the bedside table.

'What is that?'

'The key to the cottage.'

'I can't take it.'

'Why not?'

She did wish he wouldn't look so directly at people. It was intimidating.

'We don't get on.' She said it so flatly that he smiled.

'But I'm hardly ever there.'

'You don't have to do me favours just because...'

'Please take it. It would make me feel better, even if it doesn't do anything for you.'

She knew that the only way to get rid of him was to agree, so she did, and when he had gone she picked up the key and it had the address on it and the name was Curlew Cottage.

Twelve

High on the moors, where for generations men had mined coal and where his father had a drift mine, Stephen West paused. It was a perfect autumn day up there and, it being that time of year, there were no tourists or hikers, just himself, the odd bird and some sheep. He knew the cry of every bird on the fell top, he knew the different ways they flew, he could distinguish the curlew, the grouse, the sparrow hawk, the magpie.

He would shut his eyes to hear the heart-rending call of the seagulls and remember himself here as a small boy, being told by his father that they flew inland when it was going to rain. Stephen had the feeling it had more to do with the local rubbish tips, but there was no tip here, so the memory remained intact.

The grouse flew low, the partridges always seemed to be taking their families over the road when there was something coming, and lots of times he had got out and stopped the traffic to see them safely into the ditch or past the nearest gate or stone wall.

He left the car and walked across to the building which was the office. It was dark, cold and empty. He had expected at least that there would be a clerk or a secretary, his father had always employed office staff. He unlocked the door and went inside and that was a shock. It looked as though somebody had ransacked it. He remembered it in the old days, with a fire, neat, orderly and peopled. There were big heaps of papers, as though nothing was filed, the floor was greasy with dirt and there was the smell of disuse. He heard a noise at the door and turned as a man's form filled the shadows through the doorway.

'Stephen?'

'Bert?' Stephen said, recognizing him.

'Aye. I thought for a minute there it was the old man, just summat about the way you moved. How is he?'

Stephen tried to make all the right noises and failed. Bert had worked for his father for years. He was married with a grown-up daughter, Jess. Her husband, Tom Beardsley, had died recently in a train crash.

'Not so good then, eh?' Bert said helpfully. 'You here to shut things down?'

'I hope not.'

Bert's face signalled relief.

'Langstaff's gone. Just as well. There's good coal to be got out.'

'I don't know what to do.'

'You could learn and you know about offices. Work in one, don't you?'

'Not any more.'

'It all just needs taking in hand,' Bert said. Stephen thought back to that morning and his solicitor's version of things. He had gone to Sam, not just because he needed to know the legal position, but because he could tell Sam how awful everything was.

'The house is mortgaged against the business,' Sam had said. 'Your father is in debt.'

'I didn't know,' Stephen said, ashamed.

'Your parents are very proud, especially your mother. She thinks you're still three.'

That made Stephen smile, even though he didn't feel much like smiling.

'Why didn't they tell me and why didn't I come home?'

'You had your life to lead.'

'I've been wanting to come back for so long but I kept putting it off because Susan didn't want to come north. Now it seems I have the perfect excuse not to go back. I'm going to have to prop things up.' Sam said nothing. Stephen looked at him. 'Don't hold back on me. What do you think?'

'If I were you, I'd get some financial advice before you go putting money into it.'

'They're my parents. My father is dying. What am I supposed to do, see my mother on the street, the men out of work, the pit shut? Allenheads House is my mother's home and the men have families.'

Sam said nothing.

'Come on, Sam. What?'

'As your solicitor or as a friend?'

'Both.'

'As your solicitor I would advise against having anything to do with it. As your friend ... what memories do you want to be left with?'

'It's impossible,' Stephen said. 'My parents must know the business is failing. Why won't they acknowledge it? What am I supposed to do, try to hang on to the business until my father dies and lose all my money? I've worked hard for it, Sam. There's something else as well. Susan doesn't want to be here and she doesn't want me to get involved financially. She's very upset. I feel bad enough dragging her into what she thinks is the wilderness, without spending every last penny on something which seems bound to fail.'

Sam looked so hard at him that Stephen got up and wandered around the office, stopping to touch the porcelain birds on the bookcase near the window.

'What do you want to do?' Sam said.

'I don't know.'

'I think you do. I think you deliberately left London because you wanted to be here and although you think it's guilt because your father is dying perhaps it's much more deep-rooted than that. Your instincts are telling you to be here. Don't you think that's how it is?'

Stephen looked at him, smiled at him. Sam had been his best friend when they were small and he had gone through more difficulties than anybody Stephen knew.

'You always say the right thing. That's exactly how it is, Sammy.'

When Stephen had gone, Sam sat in his office and smiled. Stephen was the only person left who called him by his childhood name and it was wonderful to hear it. He had missed Stephen during all the years when Stephen had been in London, doing what seemed to him at the time to be important.

It happened to a lot of people, they came out of university and went to London as though it were the promised land and then, in time, in their thirties, they came back. London was as insular in its way as Hexham. It was just a series of small villages and he had always known that one way or another Stephen would come back here.

Who could resist it, the seashore where the waves broke high and white and the little villages where the cobles were dragged up on the sand, the fells where the air was so clear that small buildings miles and miles away were clearly defined. Stephen was not a city man, he never had been.

He had been successful, it was true, and Sam thought it must be a terrible thing to be torn between the work you loved and the land that called you. The land had won but also there was mining in Stephen's blood. Newspapers could not compete. When your ancestors had mined for 600 years, as some people in the north-east had, you could not wipe it away with intelligence and ambition, much as you might like to. It didn't work like that and in his heart Stephen West knew it.

'Your father wants you to go up,' was his mother's greeting when Stephen got home.

He plodded up the stairs. His father

looked more tired than usual, back on his pillows, his face so white and his eyes ringed dark.

'I've sorted things out legally,' he said as Stephen shut the door.

'Dad...'

His father smiled encouragingly. 'I'm very proud of you, you know, that you would give up everything you had to come back here and look after this business.'

'I was tired of London.'

'I've talked to the solicitor. He's a good lad is Sam Browne. He's not the man his father was, of course.'

'So few of us are,' Stephen said as he went downstairs.

His mother still made tea. The main meal was in the middle of the day and tea was at half past five. Stephen's insides couldn't get used to it. He and Susan had supper at eight or nine or sometimes later. When he had tea he was hungry again before he went to bed and had to resort to sneaking into the kitchen for food. Also his mother didn't have any alcohol in the house, not wine anyway, and they were used to a bottle of wine with their meal, he missed that.

He also missed his wife's cooking, his mother wouldn't let Susan do anything in the kitchen, as though she was a guest, and the cooking was old-fashioned, no garlic or Mediterranean vegetables here, and his mother's idea of going out did not include what she thought of as expensive dinners.

The days were long gone when men had needed big meals during the day because they did hard physical work, but his mother was producing meals as though they weren't. Tea was home-made baking and, although it tasted good, all the pastry and cakes and scones were enough to fatten anyone with an appetite, though Stephen had lost his somewhere between London and Newcastle and his mother complained at the little he ate.

'I never thought I'd long for a salad,' Susan said.

His mother only washed once a week, she didn't have an automatic washer, they used too much water, she said, and there was no dishwasher. Susan was allowed to wash up and sighed over her breaking nails.

'We must find somewhere to live,' she complained, 'the only time we're alone is here.'

They were in bed. The nights were frosty and so was the temperature of the house.

'I didn't expect to be here that long.'

'We could rent somewhere.'

'Renting is expensive.'

'We have capital,' Susan pointed out. 'We've just sold our house, if you remember.'

'We might need that for the business.'

Susan looked at him in the lamplight.

'My parents are almost bankrupt,' Stephen said, 'this house has a second mortgage.'

'You want us to prop up your parents and their business?'

'What else can we do?'

In the morning he was up and went to the office before Susan awoke, and that day he found a house in Burnside that somebody was moving out of, quite close to the pit. It was next door to Bert Simons in Chapel Street. He persuaded Susan to go and see it with him that afternoon. He had thought of it as ideal but when they drove up to the fells he could see that it wasn't. To a city girl like Susan this was the back end of beyond.

You could only get there by car. It had once had a railway which linked Alston and Hexham but that was gone. There were four miles of winding road up on to the moors off the main road and then you turned into the village.

The house was terraced. You couldn't get the car to the front, just the back street, the track beyond was for tractors and people only. The house was in the middle of the row. It had a back garden which Stephen judged would have been useful when people grew vegetables. It was long and narrow and the grass was high.

The view from the front windows was without equal, across the valley, past the viaduct which had once been used for the railway to carry away the coal, and then there were the woods, the fields, the sky and space. Susan stood, looking out of the sitting-room window and didn't move for what seemed to him like a long time.

'My father won't live more than a few months. I would like to help him,' Stephen said.

She turned.

'I don't know what you want any more. When we make love, I feel as though you would rather do anything else, that you just do it because you think you should. Even before you knew your father was ill, all you wanted was to leave London. It scared me, Stephen, it really did. I don't know how to please you any more. We had so much and it seems that you deliberately threw it away.'

'Nothing that mattered.'

'It did to me. We had a lovely house and a

good lifestyle and people respected you, knew who you were. Who are you here?'

'I don't care any more.'

'Do you really want us to live in this horrible little house?'

'It's either that or stay with my parents. I'm not using money that could be put to better use.'

She stared at him.

'You really are going to try and prop up the business, aren't you?'

'Yes, I am.'

She ran out of the house and slammed the door. Stephen went after her. She was crying in the garden.

'Susan, I'm sorry.'

'I don't feel I know you any more,' she said. 'I want to go back to London.'

'I can't,' he said.

'I know you can't. I know you can't leave your mother when your father is so ill, I don't expect you to. I know how I would feel if it were my parents. It's just that it's so awful here and I don't know if I can get used to it. The people here, they settle for less, they ... they don't have the same standards. I'm sorry if that sounds snobbish but they don't. They don't dress well, they don't care what their figures look like, they have different values, different ideas. I'm never going to fit here, even if I stay until I'm an old lady.'

'It won't come to that. We'll leave as soon as we can.' He didn't say 'after my father dies', because he could not imagine a world without his father. He loved Susan and she loved him but she had no experience of death. Her parents lived in a neat bungalow in Hampshire, where houses had thatched roofs, little girls had ponies and Jane Austen lived for ever. Stephen had the stupid idea that if he could have whisked his parents to Hampshire they too would have gone on. Also he felt resentful towards her – and undeservedly so, he knew – that she had kept him in London away from his parents when he should have been here. He would have come back sooner but for Susan and his love for her.

Thirteen

Jess's family had always lived in the village and she knew everybody. That should have made things easier, she felt, but it didn't. These people, she realized, were just as bad if not worse than other people at dealing with death. Some of them would cross the street so that they didn't have to speak to her, pretend they had not seen her or speak to her parents instead of to her, not looking her in the eyes. They would talk about her in the third person when she was there.

She wanted to leave her parents' house but her father and mother didn't want her to go. They were treating her as though she had not been married, as though Tom had not existed and nothing had altered. She wasn't sure how much more of it she could stand after two weeks. People had said that her feelings would change and Jess had assumed that they meant for the better, but it wasn't so, her feelings were getting worse and that was the most frightening thing of all.

After the disbelief there was the belief, the

soon-dawning awareness that Tom was dead, and it made her wish that she was dead too. Nothing occupied her, nothing helped. Their possessions had been brought back from Germany and she had not had the heart to sort through them. She left the boxes in the hall and her mother complained and that was when Jess decided that she must look for somewhere to live. She bought a car. Her father was horrified.

'They lose up to half their value in the first year. Only an idiot buys a new car.' There was worse. He told her that he would have helped, that he would have gone with her, as though she was stupid and irresponsible. When she announced that she was going to look for a house, it was as though she had committed a sin.

'Live on your own, a bit lass like you?' he said. 'Whatever would you do?'

'We like having you here,' her mother said. 'If you would just shift that stuff out of the hall.'

'I am shifting it, I'm leaving.'

'You won't go anywhere you'll be better off than here,' her mother said.

They didn't understand. How could they? She had nothing to do, nobody to be with, no place for her grief to exist.

She drove to the coast in her new car. It was a small car, she had been modest in her aspirations. Her parents had no idea how well off she was and she did not think they believed her when she tried to tell them. Tom had been generous in every way. She tried to forget him for a few minutes but there was no way her head would let her.

A thousand thousand times a day his face passed across her mind, and every part of their married life was played before her eyes like a private cinema showing. It was wearing, but not so much that she could sleep. She saw him and herself together in every place they had ever visited. It was like being haunted, possessed, as though he did not want to leave her, as though he was just out of touch, still there but unable to be seen or heard.

Jess sat on top of the sand dunes in her car and wept what felt like half a bucket of tears as she watched the tide go down. The afternoon turned quickly into evening, the days were so short. She drove a little further up past Tynemouth, the priory almost ghostly in the half-light, and then came upon some new houses which looked out over the sea. She and Tom had not lived near the sea, so it would be new, it would remind her of nothing, and she would get used to being alone in less than a million years.

People were starting to say things to her, her mother's friends and her own old friends, telling her that she would forget, saying that she would marry again. Already they had consigned Tom to history. Nobody remembered anything about him but her, and all she had were photographs and his clothes. Her mother was trying to get her to throw out his clothes, she somehow thought that would help, tried to get her to give them to a charity shop, but to her they still smelled of Tom, his expensive sweaters and shirts, his suits hanging in the wardrobe, which nightly she buried her face in.

Her mother seemed to think that the less Tom's name was mentioned the better. Jess could see that she must leave and she went up to the show house and asked the woman there for a look round.

The area was a mixture of old and new housing. There were Victorian terraces on the cliff tops, with big bay windows, and a lot of new housing which sat upon the estuary and some of it had wonderful views. There were pubs which looked as though they too had been built before the turn of the last century, there was warehousing and well-established buildings and shops, and a new hotel beside the sands, and a sailing club, and it was all so exciting.

It had a very good atmosphere, Jess thought, it was being brought up to date but in a special way, there had been a great deal of money invested here, it would be an interesting place to live.

The flat had a good view. Though the daylight had gone, she could see the lights of a ship on the horizon. The flat was on the top floor and the rooms were big. There was nothing to do but carpet, curtain and move in the furniture which she had put into storage. It had two big bedrooms, two bath-rooms, a kitchen and a big dining/living area.

It was more than enough for one person. She wrote a cheque, paid the deposit and went back to tell her parents, knowing how they would react, even pleased when they told her she could not do so. It was strange how people assumed that once your husband was dead you became a child, you could not be trusted to do anything by yourself, you could not make decisions. She also knew that in a curious way her parents had been proud and pleased that she had married a man like Tom who came from and inhabited a world they knew nothing of – culture, books, education and freedom.

They had also been pleased because they didn't have to worry about her, as if in some way he could keep her safe, though in fact he had not been able to keep himself safe. Without him they thought she was balanced precariously on some cliff edge and, out of their sight, would go over or under, somehow lose her sense of direction.

Her father shouted at her.

'You've done what?' he said.

He called her stupid. Jess told herself that it was his affection for her that made him do so, but it did not hurt any the less and she could not sustain any more hurt. She knew that her father had been poor all his life and that was why he reacted like this. He was afraid of money, having never had any. He did not want her to make mistakes, he wanted to shield her.

'You're only twenty-four,' her mother told her. She could not tell her mother that, in the few weeks since Tom died, she had aged a hundred years. She looked at people her own age, she had seen a couple walking on the beach with their arms around each other, and knew that they were a lifetime away because of her experience. She would feel more at home with old women, with those who knew what widowhood was like, because it was the only way. You had to live it to know it, her mother knew nothing. Her loss was her parents', and the more her mother said she understood, the more it hurt, because her mother already wanted her to move back, to be theirs again, wanted to claim what was left of her, and she could not do it. Her mother cried and her father raged and it only made her the more determined to get out.

Her house was not quite finished and she liked going to see the workmen as they put in the last touches. They got to know her. She wandered around the house and they would show her what they had done, proud of their work. Jess would lean on the empty window ledge and look out over the North Sea. The weather was bad. She watched the grey skies and the grey sea and the rain running down the window, and had her first moments of peace.

There was no way she would be in the house before the end of the year, so she had Christmas to get through in the village. For them it would be the same as usual and her mother had baked cakes and puddings and made plans. It didn't seem to occur to any of them that this year should be any different because Tom had died.

Last year she and Tom had spent several days alone, just the two of them, and it had been the happiest time of her life. They had done nothing, stayed in bed late, eaten good meals, drunk good wine, walked the cold city streets. Jess did her best to create some happiness for herself. She went shopping and ordered carpets and curtains. She knew that her mother was upset at not being asked to go with her, but their taste was no longer the same and she knew that she was not strong. If she took her mother she would end up with her mother's taste in furnishings.

'We won't be doing anything big for Christmas Day,' her mother assured her, 'just friends and family at home to mark the occasion.'

She was treated like a visitor, except by Tod Smith, who caught her on her own in the hall and asked whether she would like to go to bed with him, as he was sure she was missing sex. He was a neighbour, older than Jess by about four years. She laughed, it was all she could think to do, and then she went out into the back garden and cried. At least he was honest, she thought, he didn't pretend.

As often as she could, she went to her house on the seashore. What was it that was so comforting about the sea? She didn't know, only that there was silence, nobody to humour, nobody to put on a sane face for. She spent more and more time there and told nobody where she went nor invited anyone to see it. It was the only place left on earth that she felt she could exist in. It was all she could be.

Fourteen

Victoria dyed her hair pink, black and orange. She wore it crimped or corkscrewed. Caroline's mother was not convinced that the shop would like it, she certainly didn't. Caroline didn't enquire whether the shop were concerned. It obviously didn't matter too much to them, they gave her extra hours at Christmas, so she was always at work and Caroline had to be grateful for her daughter's industry. They also had free tea and coffee. Not that Caroline's mother appreciated it. She liked teabags, what Victoria scathingly called 'sweepings-up', whereas the tea she brought home smelled wonderfully of vanilla or ginger, the coffee had exotic names like St Augustin and Kenya Special Roast. It was the only luxury left, so Caroline did her best to enjoy it.

Victoria bought her mother a teapot for Christmas, covered in a banana design, it had been cheap and they got 30 per cent off, her sensible daughter told her.

Caroline's mother went to the church

Christmas dinner and had turkey. She went to visit the ladies at the chapel Christmas dinner and had turkey. She went to the WI Christmas dinner and had turkey and she went to the various carol services. She went out to tea and to sherry evenings and to sales of work and all manner of celebrations. Caroline envied her mother's ability to enjoy herself and to become involved. She stayed at home most evenings and watched television. She had discovered that she couldn't read, nor could she sit through a film. Half an hour wasted her concentration.

Victoria soon discovered a social life and Caroline was only glad. All she cared for was that they should have sufficient money for a place of their own in time and that Victoria might learn to be happy. She had stopped looking at rented property, it was so expensive. Her mother handed over the car, Caroline was pleased, at least she had some freedom. She paid the tax, insurance, maintenance and petrol. It took a great deal of money but it was worth it and she was grateful for the gift. In return, if her mother wanted taxiing anywhere, Caroline took her, but it was not often that she was stuck. She had friends with cars and was not averse to taking the bus where she needed to go, and she made the best of any outings offered.

They were invited nowhere at Christmas, as though the whole world had gone into shock. She and Michael had had a lot of friends but they were nearly all couples and they had deserted her. She had the occasional card. Worse still, some people wrote and told her, in those hideous newsletters which no doubt they sent all their friends, about their fantastic holidays, their brilliant children and their wonderful husbands.

'It makes you want to throw up, doesn't it?' Victoria observed with distaste.

Caroline worked late on Christmas Eve. Victoria and her mother were both out and the idea of going home to sit alone did not appeal. Sam and Gareth were working. At half past seven, Gareth came into her office.

'Fancy a drink?' he said.

Caroline hesitated. She still didn't like him.

'I have to get back.'

He looked sideways at her and walked out. It would have been better, Caroline thought savagely, if he had bought her a present. Sam had given Kathleen a full day at an expensive spa which must have cost him a fortune. Sam had also taken his staff out for a Christmas meal which Gareth had cried off from at the last minute. Gareth should be at home at this time on such an evening, reading his children a story and pouring his wife a gin and tonic.

Caroline slammed shut the door of the filing cabinet, switched off her computer, collected her coat and bag and went home. When she left the building the light was still burning in Sam's office. What did he do for Christmas? She had the horrible thought that he would be alone. She knocked briefly and put her head around the door.

'I'm just off.'

Sam looked up.

'Goodnight then. Have a happy Christmas.'

'What are you doing tomorrow?'

'I'm spending the day with the vicar and his wife. Pam works for me. They're nice people. They have half the parish over, a big party.'

'It sounds nice.'

'I don't really want to go,' Sam admitted. 'My brother died at Christmas last year, so I'm just going to go home and spend it quietly.'

Caroline was surprised. Sam never confided anything.

'I didn't know that. I'm so sorry. Are you sure, because–'

'Positive,' Sam said. 'Try and have a good holiday. You deserve it.'

'Thanks. Goodnight.'

The house was in darkness but when she got inside there was a yell of, 'Surprise!' and when the lights went on her mother and Victoria were waiting and her mother had made her favourite meal, strips of beef with onions, mushrooms and sour cream and mashed potatoes, and there was a good bottle of red wine to go with it. Later, when Victoria had gone to bed, she kissed her mother on the cheek and thanked her and her mother looked her straight in the eyes and said, 'You're a brave woman, Caroline. I'm so proud of you.'

Fifteen

Alex had never felt so well. She could work fifteen hours a day, eat nothing but bread and cheese, sleep for a couple of hours and then go back to work. Everybody praised her, she was in line for promotion. Then one day in early February, when she was giving a presentation to the board, she was halfway through and was beginning to feel the elation of a job well done and suddenly the words stopped.

She couldn't understand what was happening, she waited for the sound but as there was no sound there were no thoughts. She couldn't remember what she had been trying to say and when she glanced down at the few notes she had made she couldn't read them. She was sweating and the silence ticked on and her throat dried completely. She felt sick, she felt dizzy and then thankfully the floor came up to meet her and the next thing she knew she was lying down on a big leather sofa in the room next door and several people were standing over her. The chairman's secretary had a glass of water to her lips.

Alex pushed the glass away and sat up. She excused herself, said it was nothing, she had felt rather unwell the day before, and she went off to the ladies' cloakroom. There she locked herself into a cubicle just in time before the tears came. She couldn't stop them no matter how hard she tried. She went home. The tears began again and this time she let them. She went to bed, slept badly, cried again at three o'clock in the morning and the following day made an appointment to see her doctor, where she cried again.

'You're depressed,' Claire Jonason said.

'I feel fine.'

'You're not supposed to feel fine. Grieving is a process people go through, grief work. You haven't gone through it, you're avoiding it.'

'What am I meant to do, feel awful for the rest of my life?'

'It's been five months. Why don't you take some time off?'

'To do what?' Alex stared across the desk at her. 'I'm terrified, Claire,' she admitted, 'all I have is my work. If I don't have that, what am I to do?'

'Sleep, eat, rest. Try a couple of weeks at least.'

'I have too much to do.'

'You'll get worse if you don't. Then you'll be off for a lot longer or have to give up working altogether. Do you want to talk to somebody? I could–'

'I don't want pills and I don't want psychology, thank you.'

Alex went home, packed and drove to the cottage in Northumberland, arriving in the darkness, fumbling about.

The village itself was hard to find once she came off the main road, the signposts didn't seem to lead anywhere and she couldn't hear or see the sea. There were narrow roads, dark and empty, small settlements of houses, caravan parks, closed. Finally, when her strength was about gone, she came into the little village with the right name and was astonished. There in the moonlight was nothing but the odd house, a telephone box, a garage, or whatever you called it, to house the local lifeboat, rather a lot of grassy dunes, a wall or two, a pub, and at the far end of the village a road that veered off to the right.

There was a cluster of small stone houses and as she eased the car down the lane she could see the cottage itself in darkness. There was sufficient room to pull the car in behind. Dawn was arriving, at least a dim light, but nothing as spectacular as the sun, just a greying instead of darkness. She got out of the car and stilled herself.

For the first time she could hear the sea, though she couldn't see it. She found the key, fitted it into the lock and the door gave, well oiled. Just inside the hall she switched on the light. Grey carpets, white walls. A bathroom, a shower room, two bedrooms, and at the end of the hall she stepped down into a very big room and beyond it there was a huge expanse of floor surrounded by glass windows and doors. It was a sun lounge and from it and all around you could see the sea.

Alex pulled open the door and stepped outside into the morning air. There was a lawn and beyond it a tiny wall and beyond that was the seashore. The tide was full and as the dawn crept over the water she could see dozens of birds, some flying along the shore but most of them clustered as though they were at a party, black and white ducks, bobbing up and down on the water's edge, gulls and smaller birds too.

They were far enough away so that she did not disturb them, they did not heed her. It was cold there and a chilling breeze came off the sea. She stood for as long as she could bear the cold and then went back inside. As she closed the door, warm air hit her.

She took in the big sofas, wide-screen television, the hearth built up, the fire laid ready to be lit, the dining area and the kitchen, all, she had no doubt, fully equipped. The refrigerator hummed. It contained water and several bottles of champagne and when she opened the freezer everything anybody would have needed for a siege was there. She took out bread and butter, found tea and marmalade and long-life milk in the cupboards, and then she went back to the window. She boiled the kettle and heard the satisfying sound of water hitting the sides of the pot and then she sat and ate and drank and enjoyed the simple meal more than she had enjoyed anything elaborate for a very long time, and afterwards she took off most of her clothes and climbed into a comfortable double bed. By the time the pale low winter sun was making its way into the room she had gone to sleep.

Sixteen

Stephen and Susan moved next door to Bert and his family. Stephen was aware by then that Jess Beardsley was living there, but it didn't last long. He didn't blame her, he envied the kind of financial competence that would allow Jess to buy a new car and a new house without having to wait while probate was sorted out. She was beautiful in a way that a young girl sleeping rough might look, pale, pinched face, messy hair, huge brown eyes.

She didn't speak to them but he knew it was only that she did not see them or anybody. Bert and his wife were going on in the desperate hearty way that people did whose children were badly hurt. They smiled brilliantly at everybody and, even on the coldest mornings when the wind cut across the heather, Bert's wife would be out in the back garden, fighting to keep the clothes on the line. She cleaned and shopped and worked and was always going in and out of the house as though activity would mend her child's heart. Jess went out in her new little car and was gone for hours most days. When she finally left, it was like a house of mourning, the activity ceased, there was no sound of any kind through the walls.

Susan had agreed to move only when she could bear his father's illness and his mother's ways no longer and, since he had insisted they should live in the village, she went. What she did during the day he wasn't sure, convinced that when he had gone to the mine she lay in bed for hours in the mornings, watched television in the afternoons. The house was not very clean and they lived on convenience food as they had never done. He couldn't complain, he had brought her here, but it was difficult being at the mine all day when he realized he knew so little, and coming home to an uncomfortable draughty little house, meals where the bland food tasted of nothing and a wife who had nothing to say or to offer.

Stephen soon realized that it had been a mistake to live among the people who worked for him. They regarded him from suspicious eyes, as well they might, they all seemed to know more than he did about mining. He was to them, in spite of having been brought up here, a southerner, a foreigner, a man who had come into something which was ailing, armed with nothing but his ignorance. He couldn't afford to pay a manager, so he struggled and the miners watched him struggling and didn't help.

He knew that they had nicknamed him 'the office boy'. He longed to go to the pub in the village but he couldn't because they drank there. If he wanted a pint after work he had to drive out of the village to the Cross Keys, several miles up on the moors, and it was lonely. He had been away too long, he had no friends and he couldn't have much to drink because he had to drive back.

Occasionally, when he couldn't stand the idea of going home to Susan, he telephoned and said he was staying, and drank himself happy there by an open fire. It was the only pleasure he had left. She didn't seem to care whether he came home. She was all cold disapproval, as though there was something more to be done.

The pitmen themselves, many of them, were older than him, had been with the pit all their working lives. In particular there were the four Elliot brothers, who lived at the bottom of the village. There had been five brothers in all; their parents had both been drunks.

138

The oldest one was Philip, but it was the second son, Matthew, who had left and become rich. The other four stayed, worked and had children. They were unfriendly to the point where Stephen didn't know what to say. Bert would have been more help, Stephen thought, if he had been able, but he was so worried about his daughter and the effect that Jess's unhappiness was having on his wife that he seemed to have nothing left to offer and went to work silently each day with his head down.

One March evening when Stephen had called in to see his father after work, his mother told him that she wanted to talk to him and, before he left, he went into the kitchen. It had always been his favourite room, the old cream Aga, the view of the back garden, the pots and pans, the memories of his mother making meals and his father pouring sherry when he was a little boy.

'You and Susan must move back in here when your father's gone, and I'll find something in the village,' she said. 'It won't be long. I think we ought to try and organize something. It would give me something to do.'

'Move in?'

'It's far too big for me. Presumably you intend to have children, it's not for me to tell you these things, but this house is ideal for a family. I'll be quite happy in a little house nearby.'

Little houses in Hexham were expensive.

'Mother, there isn't any money for another house just at present.'

'Nonsense, you'll have this. You can afford a small place for me.'

'The business is badly in debt and every penny I have is going there.'

'In debt?' She stared at him. 'Nobody in our family has ever been in debt.'

'The business is in a bad way, surely you understand that.'

'Why, what have you done to it? It always did make money. Your father said to me, there is nothing to worry about, Stephen will come home and run the business. I'm sure you'll be able to organize things.'

'Did my mother speak to you about us moving back there after my father dies?' he asked when he got back to the cottage.

'I think she wants it sorting out, presumably it's less complicated legally. I don't know. It sounds like a good idea to me.'

'We can't have it.'

'It's a very nice house. You were the one who wanted to leave London. Surely you don't expect me to stay in this hencoop after your father dies. When I married you, you were a respected member of a decent profession, you had a good income, we had a lovely home, went to the theatre and the opera and for holidays in exciting places. Now what have we got, nothing to look forward to but your mother's company and your father's–'

Stephen walked out. He drove up on to the moors and stopped the car and remembered all those times being with his dad up on the fell. It was his father's world up there, he would point out the birds by name and show Stephen the bees in the bell heather in August. In high summer the fells were purple with it, cloaked in it, rich and high. In winter the whiteness of the snow seemed to go on for ever.

His dad would go out all day with him and take the spaniels, and they would walk with guns and perhaps come upon one pheasant and proudly take that home. It was hard, that was what his dad had liked most about it, it was a hard living from a hard land. He knew very well that his father could bear no less, some men were built like that, and he knew also that, although his dad had been pleased to give him a university education and watch him go to London and work for a top newspaper, it was not really what his dad would have wanted most.

He had seen them in his mind working here together, he had seen Stephen like this with rough dirty hands. Men's work. It was stupid, Stephen knew, it didn't matter any more, men didn't have to do such things to be men, and yet he knew that his father believed anybody could make a living in a place like London, all you needed was your wits and education, but here only those who bettered nature and took like thieves and were cunning like snipers could do it, and it was a matter of pride to his father, the little old man at home in bed.

That evening when he went back to the house, the moment he entered, the sounds and sights and smells were all of times long ago. His father and mother had not altered so much as a chair's position in thirty years. The Aga was warm in the kitchen, the kettle was boiling. There were freshly baked cakes cooling on the wire rack, dough bases, jam in the middle and sweet sponge on top.

His mother busied about in the kitchen, because, she said, his father was sleeping.

He refused tea and cake and went into the sitting room. This room was now a bedroom for his father, it was easier than having the doctor and the nurse and his mother running up and down stairs. It had the view. It had big French windows and looked out across the gardens where he had played as a child and past the fields to where the hills rose towards the fells and, further over, though you couldn't see it from here, was the pit which was his father's.

As he stood there looking at the shadows, he heard a stirring from the bed and his father's voice, slight, as it had never been. He went over and sat down in the chair which was always by the bed. This was the room that was different. In here on Sunday afternoons he and his dad had watched television, had helped John Wayne to save the world. On Saturdays his dad would take him to the pictures and was often so tired that he fell asleep and snored and Stephen would shrink into his seat in embarrassment.

His father should have been in hospital, Stephen knew, but his parents would not have that, so he stayed here, drugged for the pain. He wanted to die here and, if you had to die, you couldn't have a better place to do it in, unless you could have managed the walk up to the top of the fells.

Each day, his father wanted to hear all about the pit, and Stephen tried not to tell him about the financial problems. It would not have helped for him to know that the business was in the kind of trouble it was unlikely to emerge from. He talked about the wildlife he had seen and the way that the wind bit its road across the level ground and he knew that his father could close his eyes and picture himself there.

'Stephen, I want to say something to you.'

'Anything.'

'I'm glad you came home. That isn't what I wanted to say. I want you to... When it's all over, I want to be up there, on my own ground, I want my ashes scattered across the fell tops. Your mother is all for burial. I don't want that.'

'Have you told her?'

'I tried to. She has some foolish notion that buried people are still there and although I would do a great deal to comfort her–' he smiled – 'I have no inclination to spend time in a cemetery. No graves, eh?'

What a mess death was, Stephen thought, and how much the Lord expected of people that they should face it with some form of courage. God didn't deserve people.

'Don't worry, I'll sort it,' he said.

The effort seemed to have exhausted his father. He went to sleep.

Seventeen

Alex awoke in the middle of the night and
broke into a sweat. There was a noise outside
and it was definitely the noise of somebody
rather than something. She thought that she
had heard a car but that had gone, footsteps
and then a key in the lock and she put on a
dressing gown and switched on the lights
just in time to see Matthew as he walked into
the hall with a bag of some kind. Alex didn't
know what to say. He could have had no idea
that she was here. She clasped the dressing
gown closer with her fingers and said, 'I'll go
to a hotel.'

'Don't be silly,' he said gently. 'Go back to
bed.'

He didn't linger. He took his case and
went along the hall.

Alex went back to bed. She was very tired.
He made no more noise, so she slept. It was
strangely comforting to have another person
in the house. She slept late but, when she
was sitting having breakfast at about half
past nine, he appeared, wearing jeans and a

146

sweater and looking quite different from how she had seen him before, more relaxed.

'I should have let you know I was here,' she said.

'The place is big enough for two of us, surely.'

He made bacon sandwiches. Alex refused and then wished she hadn't, the smell was wonderful. The day was grim, it rained hard, with a wind behind it. She went back to bed with a book, heard music coming from the sitting room and, when she got up again after one, he had made lunch, lit the fire, offered her wine. She hadn't thought he was in the least domesticated, she was quite sure that at home he had a housekeeper and a driver and presumably people to do all those things. Nobody said much but Alex didn't feel uncomfortable. She accepted food and wine and even sat by the fire in an easy chair as the short day closed in. The television was on, so she didn't have to attempt conversation. To her astonishment, he went to sleep, lying on the sofa. She would not have done such a thing in the company of someone whom she considered to be her enemy.

She glanced at him and then back at the television and then at him again in case he was pretending, but he wasn't, he was completely deeply asleep, his face softened by the thick fringe of his lashes. She went back to watching the film but she couldn't concentrate on it. So this, Alex thought, lying on the rug by the fire, was what he was privately like, except that the man who was asleep on the sofa was the kind of man who no woman in her right mind would ever marry, though plenty would have said yes.

He would never be easy to be with, he was ambitious, ruthless, difficult and few people had ever seen him like this. He had been a bad husband and worse father and all his money and ability could not make up for that. Yet the only reason she was here was because he considered her family, and he was the one man she could bear to be with. She was protected from him by himself, his loyalty to his son made him feel responsible for her, he wouldn't harm or endanger her. Alex hadn't felt safe with a man before, hadn't needed to, or was it just that she hadn't allowed herself to, because it showed her vulnerability? She didn't hate him any more.

That was a shock, she needed to hate him, to have somebody to blame, to lash out at. Worse still, she was conscious of him, not as Andrew's father, but as a man, more attractive somehow than Andrew or Tom had been, and it was not just his money, it was his body, which was in nice shape. Alex bounced up and shot out of the room. She had been alone too long, she thought, to consider him in such a light.

She stayed in her room until she was thoroughly tired of it and could smell dinner. She crept along the hall and into the sitting room and he was there without the benefit of lights, television or music. He switched on a small lamp beside him when he heard her. She accepted a glass of wine and when he sat down again she said, 'Did you bring Margaret here?'

'Only once. She couldn't see the point of it.'

'Andrew?'

'He didn't like it. There's nothing here for children.'

'Children don't need a lot, they just need parents to be with them.'

Matthew looked at her.

'OK, so I was terrible at parenting.'

'Why?'

'I was always at work.'

It was a good enough reason, plenty of less successful men would have said the same thing, but to her it didn't ring true.

'Why don't you just tell me the truth, there's nobody here but us, and it can't hurt either of them,' she said. 'Didn't you love Margaret?'

'Yes.'

'But you went around with other women, and not just one or two–'

'She didn't love me. I don't think she ever loved me.'

'You got married because she was pregnant.'

'Yes.'

He didn't say anything else and Alex listened to the winter sea, crashing itself off the rocks at the top of the beach.

'Did you resent having to marry her?'

'I didn't have to marry her.' Alex stared at him. 'Andrew wasn't mine.'

'He wasn't your son?'

'No.'

'How on earth could you know that?'

'Because I can't have children.'

She didn't know what to say to that.

'But you wouldn't know that then. You thought he was yours.'

'Andrew was her father's child. I married her to get her out of there and ultimately to get us both out of the village.'

They sat in silence for so long that he got

up abruptly and went into the kitchen, taking the glasses with him and refilling them. She followed him there.

'You must have resented it then.'

'It wasn't that so much, it was just that I couldn't manage it all. She didn't ever want to go to bed with me, because of him, and Andrew became the only person she cared about. She suffocated him and ... I was jealous. Isn't that awful, to be jealous of a child, especially a child who thought you were his parent. I thought if I made a lot of money it would get better. Wasn't that ridiculous? I was too young to know. I wanted to give her everything and she didn't want any of it and she didn't want me.'

There was something about his back, because he was turned away, something defenceless. Alex was silenced, had a terrible desire to put her arms around him and it was not a carnal thing, she wanted to protect him. How utterly ridiculous, when he was so controlled and so sure of himself that he terrified other people. She was flattered too that he had told her these things which she felt sure he had not told anybody else. Why did he trust her, confide in her? She couldn't understand.

It was not that he wanted her, she knew

151

when men did, so many had. How strange when they were not, even because of Andrew, related in any way, he treated her with a kind of respect no man had ever done. It was almost like the kind of pure love between a parent and a child, though which was which she could not have distinguished. Perhaps it was just that neither of them had anybody. Whatever, she was convinced it was the longest utterance of his life and she was rather pleased.

He picked up both glasses and turned to her and smiled and gave her a glass and he said, 'What about some dinner?' and they didn't discuss it any more.

Eighteen

Jess moved before Easter. She went to live in her house by the seashore. What was it that was so comforting? She didn't know, only that there was silence, nobody to humour, nobody to pretend to, to put on a front for. She bought an answering machine with the telephone, put it on, locked the doors, had a bath, switched on the television, wrapped herself in a dressing gown and sat down and watched television. She watched it every day for every waking hour.

She went to her local supermarket and bought a lot of food and a lot of wine and then she went home and locked the doors again and for a month she didn't go out except to her video store, and even that stopped when a man with a van brought videos to the door. He was Jess's saviour, her Jesus, her Messiah, her Buddha. He was Santa Claus, a chubby man with a van load of goodies. She could be somewhere else, she could be somebody else, she could be a story.

153

Sometimes she watched the same video three or four times and each time it gave her something different. It was wonderful, it had a beginning, a middle and an end, things were resolved, they were sorted out, the messiness only occurred in the middle and you could watch the different plots, the threads being gathered up at the end, and it was so clever.

She couldn't read, the words danced, moved, meant nothing. She could not gather her mind sufficiently to make the distance between herself, the writer and the words, but with television, with videos – they said watching was the nearest thing to death – she wanted to be as close as she could, to breathe the very air.

She clung to her the teddy bear which Tom had given her last Christmas. It was ginger with moving arms and legs and head. She sat hour upon hour undisturbed in the quiet, with the bear against her, and watched the flickering screen and drank her wine and ate all manner of delicacies. Time stopped. There was no world outside, nothing but the ever-changing sea, which rolled out but comfortingly rolled back in and then back out, so that you always knew where you were.

It snowed. Jess walked the long wide Northumbrian beach, where thousands upon thousands of people had left their footprints in the sand. Daily the tide took away any evidence, nothing was left upon the clean, wet beach. Jess loved the darkness, she gloried in the crashing winter tides, opened her windows when she went to bed at night – though in truth it was never before three, when the darkness had been around for half the day – and she could hear the reassuring sound of the breakers, sometimes with the wind screaming behind them.

Her parents left messages on the answering machine, so that Jess stopped playing it back, and sometimes people buzzed the intercom but she knew they couldn't get to her. She closed the curtains and bolted the windows. Nothing could come close, nothing could interfere. The post backed up behind the door.

Each morning she had a hangover. It wasn't a bad hangover, it was the evidence of wine drunk too quickly. It was not so bad a hangover that she couldn't start drinking again at lunchtime.

She sorted her wines carefully and discovered what she liked and had them at exactly the right temperature. She had good coffee and tea, chose them especially, and her life became a routine, breakfast at nine, coffee at eleven, lunch at one, tea at four, and sometimes she watched the quiz shows. She had a newspaper delivered and did crosswords and carefully worked out her evening's entertainment. She began to read. She discovered Jane Austen. What a strange world. Nobody died and nothing happened. People picked strawberries and drank tea and made conversation such as was never made but in the clever woman's mind. Jess ventured to her library and then spent hours in bookshops and borrowed and bought other books. In the afternoons she would go for long walks and then settle down on the sofa with a book and a box of Thornton's chocolates.

By six o'clock it was dark and the magic of the evening began. She would have duck and plum sauce with pancakes for dinner, or lamb with rosemary or pork with cream and mushrooms, and at half past seven the video of the evening would start.

By seven o'clock the wine bottle would be opened and Jess could taste the fullness of the grapes, the blackberries, the goose-berries, it was almost like being a child let loose in a sweet shop. If she drank enough, she could listen to music, not popular music, classical stuff, she didn't know anything about it but if you drank enough you could understand.

She got up one day before lunch and decided to sort out the post and there she found a letter from Sam Browne dated several weeks earlier, saying that things ought to be put into her name now that probate was through, and he needed to see her and she might want to speak to a financial advisor. Jess was starting to run out of cash, so she telephoned and made an appointment with him and the following Wednesday she got dressed and drove up the Tyne Valley to Sam's office.

It was a cold day. Jess wore a thick coat and cursed that she couldn't park anywhere near and had to walk up the steep hill amongst the other people. She kept her head down and turned in at the gate which led to the garden and then up the steps into the waiting area of Sam's office. She was on time and was ushered almost immediately up the stairs.

She didn't even have time to read anything about sheep or choose herself a holiday cottage with a drive of cobblestones and cow shit. The view beyond Sam's window, all sheep and hay and stone walls and snow, was so bloody wonderful that it made her want to throw up, and Sam greeted her, as no doubt he greeted everybody, as though it had made his day that she had bothered to turn up.

She watched the sheep tucking into hay as she would a box of chocolates, sat down and signed whatever had to be signed and half-listened as Sam droned on and on about what she ought to do with her money and the man she should go and see unless she had ideas of her own. She quite liked listening to the comforting sound of his voice. Finally, business over, Sam sat back in his chair.

'So, how are you?'

Jess gazed out of the window. She wouldn't make it back in time for lunch, nor the Chardonnay she had put into the fridge, though in truth it was cold for white wine. She imagined how it would be in the summer, sitting on her balcony, drinking the cool wine in the warm day. She would forget about that. When she got back she would open a bottle of Medoc. She had some particularly good cheese—

'I had your father here the other day, wanting to know what you were doing,' Sam said.

Jess pulled her gaze back to him.

'What made him think you would know?'

Sam smiled.

'Solicitors know everything,' he said.

'Only in hell,' Jess said, getting up and going to the window, the better to see the sheep and avoid Sam's gaze.

'Is that what this is?'

Jess turned and she smiled back at him.

'It's Hexham, Sam. Try to keep a sense of proportion.'

He got up and went to her.

'They're worried about you. You don't answer their phone calls or your door and you don't visit them.'

'They were so worried about me that they celebrated Christmas. Do you know what that's like? My mother made Christmas puddings and cakes. The house was full of the smell. Last Christmas...'

'What was last Christmas like?'

'It was the last Christmas,' Jess said softly.

'We're celebrating Gareth's birthday next week,' Sam said. 'Why don't you come?'

'I don't want parties.'

'You could just be there. Saturday, eight, at his house.'

Jess didn't answer. She swept out of his office. She was back in time for a late lunch and to watch the snow dissolve itself into

159

rain. There wasn't much. It didn't ever snow properly at the seaside, she had discovered. She locked the doors and got out the wine and when the afternoon was almost over she pulled the curtains shut and closed out everybody and everything.

Safe and warm, Jess listened to her favourite sounds, the ocean, the wine as it poured into her glass. On her television screen, Bruce Willis was saving the world and she could help him. By the end of the afternoon they had put everything back to rights. It was so satisfying. The baddies died, the goodies were saved. Bruce Willis's character went home to his wife and children. Jess watched him, she watched his car as it got smaller and smaller on the screen. He and his wife, sitting in the back seat, going home to their children, their house, their Christmas.

Nineteen

'You'll have to get married again,' Caroline's mother announced one Saturday morning over breakfast. 'You're no good on your own. I knew you wouldn't be. You don't earn enough money to keep you and Victoria and you'll never make enough for a house of your own. You can stay here of course for as long as you like–'

'I am not going to get married.'

'Caroline, you cannot afford to be choosy. You need to marry and if you can possibly manage it at the age of forty you need to marry well, money in fact. You made a mess of it the first time in that respect and now you need to get it right. We are long livers in our family. What are you going to do, stay poverty-stricken for the next forty years?'

'It won't be like that.'

'Won't it? Don't you ever meet a nice man at that solicitor's? That Browne man, he isn't married. Smile at him. Buy a short skirt. Have your hair done. Do something,' her mother said and began to clear the breakfast table.

Caroline joined a singles club. She was amazed at herself for doing such a thing, but when she telephoned to enquire, a man on the other end of the phone sounded so cheerful and young that she was encouraged. There was a monthly magazine which had notices in it saying things like, 'Hi, I'm Anne and I'm a young fifty-three. I'm looking forward to meeting everyone in my area. I like swimming, hiking and computer games. Give me a ring. My telephone number is...' and so on.

Caroline couldn't imagine herself writing anything. She decided instead, after she had paid her one hundred pounds (a hundred pounds!), to contact her local go-between and see when the next pub meet-up was. He told her that the next one was an under-forties, so that was no good to her, but the evening after that there was a general pub meeting. She decided to go along. Her mother encouraged her. She didn't tell Victoria, who would have been mortified at the uncoolness of it.

Caroline had forgotten how long it took to get ready to go out, hair-washing, bath, make-up, deciding what to wear, fitting her feet into high-heeled shoes – had she really worn things like this? Most of her clothes didn't fit, she was much thinner, she thought in despair, her shape had altered and not for the better, it was not slimness – she looked haggard, tired, drawn, older. She saw someone else when she looked into the mirror, and she was not sure that it was someone she liked, or that anybody else might like.

She drove to Newcastle, spent ages looking for a parking space, and then had a long walk to the pub. The meeting was in an upstairs bar, a long narrow room, and as soon as she went in she could see that there were a lot more women than men. Several women aged about sixty were sitting down, so she went to join them. Sitting down, she realized afterwards, was a mistake. You couldn't approach other people and they couldn't approach you. The women were talking about their operations, their illnesses past and present. The men were standing at the bar and, from what she could hear, they were discussing next week's ramble and the party which Vicky was having, a fork and plate party.

'What's a fork and plate party?' Caroline ventured.

'Oh, you take food,' a young man near her said. 'Come and be introduced.'

There was one good-looking man of about her age standing at the bar though he wouldn't have been noticed if Gareth Forester had been anywhere around, Caroline thought, smugly, as though she partly owned Gareth.

He was new. Nobody introduced them and he didn't look at her. He began talking to two younger women, Caroline judged them to be less than thirty. They had short skirts, lots of make-up, short hair, long earrings and loud laughs. She felt very old. A tubby man introduced her to a pale thin young woman. Caroline, when asked, had told him she was widowed.

'This is Moira,' he said, 'her husband committed suicide.'

At half past ten, Caroline slunk into the night, drove home as fast as she dared and tiptoed into the house. Luckily her mother had gone to bed, not waited up for a report on the evening. She put on her dressing gown, switched on the television and opened a bottle of wine. Oh, the relief of not having to talk, the peace of the house, the ease of the television. She felt as though she had just taken part in something which took all your strength, like being an enemy agent in another country or a spy in the war. She didn't even have to turn a page. Some chat-show host was putting somebody's world back to rights. Caroline was glad.

She went to a party in a block of flats in a bad part of the city. She wondered whether her car wheels would be there when she came out. The man whose flat it was talked to her about books because she was early. Caroline was almost happy and then lots of people arrived and he had to provide curry. A tall man in a dark coat asked her to marry him and later she danced with a short bald man who told her that he was a lighthouse keeper. Caroline thought he was drunk. There was another party the following week. Caroline said she would go. There would be music.

At half past twelve, despite their protest-ations, Caroline left. Not many lights were unsmashed outside and she lost her way among the steps and alleyways, but to her relief her car was untouched. She drove home at breakneck speed. Her mother was waiting up.

'I don't think I can stand another night,' Caroline said.

'But it was so expensive,' her mother said, 'and you did say there was a party.'

The next party was in a hotel, it was a

dinner dance. Caroline bought herself an expensive new dress, white, which she thought looked good. When she sat down to eat at one of the long tables, she thought longingly of Michael and the many meals which he had bought her in wonderful restaurants. There was tinned grapefruit, overdone beef and chocolate fudge cake you could have stotted off the floor. Caroline ate nothing, the food would not go down and the wine was so cheap that it gave her mouth a shock.

After dinner there was dancing. At her table was a tall, fair, handsome man. He leaned over and Caroline waited for him to ask her to dance.

'You ought to get yourself a man and quickly,' he said, 'by the time you're fifty there are twice as many available women as available men,' and he turned to the woman on his right and asked her to dance.

After that Caroline did not go out again. Her invisibility to other people made her feel vulnerable.

'You'll never get a man sitting at home,' her mother said. Weekends were the worst, she was never invited anywhere, and after she had contacted old friends and asked them for Sunday lunch and not been asked back, she gave up on them. That Tuesday Sam said as he passed her desk, 'Gareth's thirty-fifth is on Saturday. You're invited, if you'd like to come.'

She knew it was not a special invitation, everybody had been asked, but at least she would know somebody. She said that she would.

Caroline was half-inclined to cry off, she hated walking into places by herself, but her mother had gone to visit friends who lived in Palma and Victoria was spending the weekend with somebody from work and was going to a party, so she felt particularly left out. She would know Ivy, the receptionist from the office, and Kathleen, Sam's secretary, and Gareth and Sam. She could not spend the rest of her life alone at home, though she badly wanted to. She was going to wear her white dress but Victoria said it made her look like the world's oldest bride, so she hastily took it off again and put on a black skirt and low-necked black top which even her daughter approved of. Her mother was always pleased when she was going out, saying before she left for Majorca, 'Stick to Sam Browne, he's the man for you.'

Gareth's house was large, detached, in its

own grounds. The rumour was that his wife's family had money. Caroline felt quite sick but, when she had parked the car amongst a lot of glamorous vehicles, she spotted Sam's ancient Land Rover and felt better. She went inside, found Ivy and Kathleen standing by the buffet table, and took refuge with them. They chatted, people arrived. After a short while Kathleen's gaze made its way over her shoulder, eyes fixed. Caroline turned.

'Now that's what I call the real thing,' Kathleen said.

There was nothing about him, Caroline thought at first, you wouldn't have said he was good-looking or particularly striking, but he had what her father used to call 'presence'. He wasn't young and he didn't look women up and down like Gareth did, there was just something about him which pleased.

'Who is it?' Caroline ventured.

'Don't you know Matthew Elliot when you see him? I thought everybody did. Just think of all that money.'

'Who's the woman?'

'His son's widow.'

'His son's bit of stuff,' Ivy contributed. 'They were never married.'

'It doesn't matter these days, Ivy, they lived together.'

'It isn't the same thing,' Ivy said.

A young woman had come across. She was tall and slender and had eyes you might have fallen into, Caroline thought.

'I'm Jess Beardsley. We met once in Frankfurt,' she said to Caroline.

Caroline hugged her. She didn't ever hug people she barely knew, but somehow Jess looked as though she might fall over if somebody didn't. Jess didn't talk. She hovered as though she needed somewhere to be, and she put away a lot of wine, Caroline thought, though it didn't seem to affect her speech or her stance. Caroline wondered whether she was driving.

Sam was there and Caroline had been surprised, because she knew, as everybody knew, that Sam never went to parties. He was a loner. Every time she glanced across, he was with somebody else, as though it was business. He talked little and smiled politely just like he did at the office.

Caroline tried not to envy Gareth's wife. After all, he went with other women, but Sylvia was pretty, young, blonde, had two children. Caroline had caught glimpses of them in their pyjamas at the head of the stairs. The house was lavishly furnished, well heated, just the kind of house that most women wanted, with big gardens, a huge hall, large reception rooms, a kitchen with a blue Aga, a utility room bigger than most people's kitchens and a great sweeping staircase.

Gareth didn't even speak to Caroline. Later, people danced but nobody asked her. She wandered about the downstairs of the house. Snow had begun to fall heavily as it so often did when Easter approached. The other women from the office went home. Caroline decided it was late enough and went in search of her host or hostess to thank them and leave. She ventured into the kitchen and was just in time to see Susan West smack her husband across the mouth. They had not been introduced but Ivy had pointed them out earlier. Things were not going well, Caroline surmised, as Susan West swept past her and slammed the door, leaving her alone in the kitchen with a man she did not know.

There was only one word to describe Stephen West, Caroline thought. He was gorgeous, dark brown eyes and hair that was pale blond. She should have gone back out but somehow she couldn't go and leave him there, leaning back against the sink unit, hands clenched at either side and head lowered.

The girl was watching Matthew from across the room almost as though she recognized him. He had seen her when he walked in. She was beautiful in a rare kind of way, with short dark hair pushed behind her ears and a skin which had just missed freckles. She was very young. There was something appealing about her. She wore a plain black dress and no jewellery, no make-up, nothing to attract. She was not smiling but was standing alone, as though there was an invisible line which she would let no one cross. She was drunk. He had seen his parents drunk too often not to recognize it, though he wasn't sure what gave her away. He went to her.

'Hello. I'm Matthew Elliot. Would you like to dance?'

She didn't say anything but she let him lead her gently towards the parquet floor and take her into his arms.

In all the aching time since Tom had died, Jess had felt as though she was standing on the edge of a very deep, very dark lake, but when she began to dance with Matthew Elliot it was as though inside her head she

171

took a step back. It was a strange feeling. He held her close but it was not the way in which other men had, so that they could feel more of her body better. He held her close against the night and against the intrusion of other people's clumsiness and against the emptiness of the doorway, which Tom did not fill.

Her instincts told her that this man could shield her from the devils which beset her mind night after night. They didn't talk and the music seemed far away. It took with it the immediacy of Tom's absence and all the days since, with their top-quality nightmare. The horror had momentarily stopped. It was like waking up, realizing that the whole thing was only a bad dream. Daylight would arrive, the world would turn. Tom would come home.

The music ceased and filled the air with great silence. Jess wanted to cling. Luckily it started again almost immediately. She closed her eyes against him. It was like peering out of her hiding place for the first time. All too soon the music stopped again. When she opened her eyes he had danced her out of the room and into the huge, empty conservatory.

Conservatories always seemed to Jess the

kind of places where you grew things, but people didn't, they filled them up with cane furniture and wall lights and this one had furniture pushed to the far walls. There were candles which reflected back through the double glazing. Jess would have suspected any other man of dancing her there for ill purposes, but nothing happened. The music went on in the distance, she put her arms around his neck and leaned against him and they went on dancing. He held back the darkness with his body.

Matthew had approached Stephen earlier.

'Sorry to hear your father is so ill,' he said.

Stephen was wishing himself a long way away. Susan had looked at the house with envious eyes and was barely speaking to him. This was what she wanted and he was busy putting their capital into the pit. He could not even remember what they had quarrelled about, just that he drank rather a lot because she was driving and because everything was so difficult and she hated it when he drank.

Stephen and Matthew knew one another slightly. Matthew had left Burnside when Stephen was a very small child, and Stephen knew that his parents considered Matthew to be an upstart. He remembered, or did he, his mother saying that Matthew had once come to the house with a message from his father at the pit and been told off for coming to the front door. She referred to him now as 'that man' and, although his brothers were hard-working decent people with wives and families, his parents remembered Bill Elliot and his wife. She was dirty, which was an unforgivable thing in a pit village, and they were both heavy drinkers.

Stephen remembered that Matthew hardly went to school, that he was sly and foul-mouthed and sharp-eyed and he had done the one thing a boy should not. He had got a local girl pregnant when he was sixteen and had to marry her. Both the girl and the child were dead now.

'How's it going at the pit? Will you shut it down?'

'I don't know yet.'

'Might you be interested in selling it?'

'Selling?'

'If it comes to the point where you think of closing or selling, you could give me a call.'

'What would you do with a pit?' Stephen couldn't help asking.

'It's a business like any other,' Matthew said coolly and Stephen was irked and remembered why people didn't like him. He made you feel incompetent, as though he could do much better, and of course it was true, which made it worse.

'It loses money,' he said.

'If it had sufficient capital investment, it could be helped out.'

Stephen shook his head.

'My parents would never sell it.'

'If they change their minds, you could let me know.'

Sam remembered now why he didn't go to parties. He had heard doctors say that everybody told them their illnesses. This evening everybody had a legal problem which they wanted his opinion on and several of them came up to him and asked him when they could see him, and Sam was too polite to tell them that they should just phone the office. Not content with that, they kept telling him the problems as though he went to parties for no other reason than for it to be just like work.

He glanced over at Caroline several times. He had come to the party with the idea that he might take all his courage and ask her to dance with him, but somehow every time he almost got across the room, somebody accosted him yet again. It was therefore late when he began looking for her.

The party and other people were not wholly to blame, he knew. He was not used to asking anybody to dance. He was not used to wanting to ask anybody. He had thought he was happy at the farm and at his work. He was afraid that this was no longer completely true. Before, when he had been attracted to women, it just took a few memories of how he and Jo had fought, with Dominic in the middle, to stop him from going further. This time it didn't work. He presumed that the more used he got to seeing Caroline at work, the less he would want her, but just now that wasn't true and he searched the house.

'Looking for anybody in particular?' Gareth said.

'I just wondered where the others were, Ivy and—'

'Kathleen and Ivy left a while since.' Gareth smiled and moved close, so that he could talk into Sam's ear. 'And the beautiful Caroline left with another woman's husband. Shall I tell you who it was?'

From the back of the house, Caroline had heard a car start up, rev hard and scream away through the snow.

Stephen West lifted his head.

'Sorry,' he apologized.

His mouth was bleeding. Caroline feared for the collar of his white shirt. She gave him some tissues from her handbag. In her haste, Susan West had brought the beautiful diamond ring across her husband's mouth, Caroline thought, having noted the jewel with some envy. It took style to backhand a man like that. Stephen West was rather drunk. Caroline imagined the time when he had given his wife such an exquisite ring. Susan West wore an expensive dress, drove what sounded like a sports car and had walked in on the arm of this very stylish man. What on earth had they quarrelled about?

The bleeding stopped, it was just the side of his mouth. He was younger than Caroline by five or six years, she thought.

'I'm just leaving. Do you want a lift home?' she asked politely.

'I'm sure it's too far out of your way.'

'It doesn't matter,' she said.

They left by the back door, as his wife had. Already the tracks which the car had made were being covered with snow. He gave directions and he was right, it was the opposite way. Perhaps, had he not been drunk, he wouldn't have let her do it, or was it just that he preferred his friends not to know that his wife had left him there in such a fashion?

The snow got worse until Caroline could hardly see, in spite of the wipers going as fast as they would. Five or six miles into the country and then they reached the tiny village where a couple of street lamps were the only help. Caroline knew the place well, Michael had come from there, and when they were young they had gone for walks in the country around it and kissed in the woods.

'Where is it?' she said.

'Further along on the left. I shouldn't have dragged you out here.' He sounded more sober. 'You can't take the car any further.' Caroline stopped the car rather than parked it. 'You'll never make it back,' he said.

He was right, she thought. It was one thing driving in snow with somebody else, it was another on your own, so she got out, locked the car and waded through several inches of snow down the back lane into the yard and then to the door. There was no sign of a car.

Inside, the house was cool and it was

barely furnished. There was oilcloth on the kitchen floor. He filled the kettle and went into the other room and put a match to the ready-laid fire. There was a carpet in that room but it had seen wear and the armchairs were threadbare. He went back into the kitchen and made coffee while Caroline put her hands up to the tiny amount of warmth coming from the fire. When he came back she took the hot cup gratefully.

'This is your house?'

He smiled ruefully.

'No, it's just somewhere to live while I ... sort things out.'

'Your wife...?'

'She probably went to my parents' house, which is on the edge of the town.' He sat down on the chair, Caroline took the sofa. 'Is it Sam you know or Gareth?'

'I work for Gareth.'

'Lucky you.'

Caroline enjoyed the real fire, she hadn't seen one in ages. Soon it was warm enough to sit well back in her chair. It was strange being alone with a man and she could see that he was upset, worried, the strained look on his face belied his years.

'Divorced?' he said.

'No, my husband died.'

'How awful. What happened?'

Caroline was quite surprised at this, people didn't ask, men especially. She found herself telling him, while he prompted her from time to time, his face not just polite with interest as people usually were if she talked too much about Michael, and then she remembered that Stephen West had been a journalist. He knew exactly what to ask, when to show sympathy. She related the story of Michael's redundancy and how he had not told her.

'My father's doing something like that,' Stephen offered. 'He's going bankrupt, dying of cancer, and he won't acknowledge that the business isn't fine when in fact he's been struggling with it for years. He's going to lose his life and if we aren't careful my mother will lose her home and fifty men their jobs.'

Caroline watched him. It was pleasant to have the attention of a nice man. She hardly dared look at him, getting more sober by the minute. She liked his hands, they were writer's hands, slender, with long fingers. The only man she had been this close to lately was her dentist.

It made her think of Michael and how lucky Susan West and women like her were.

They could not imagine, had not needed to, what it was like to be without. If they had only known about cold, lonely beds, waking up by yourself, struggling with everything, Susan West would not have hit her husband across the face like that, no matter what his faults. He had deprived her of London, brought her to this place. Dear, dear. What children such women were, some man had taken away their toys and expected them to behave like adults.

'Did she have a career?'

'What?'

'Your wife. Did she have a job she loved and didn't want to give up?'

'No, but you have to admit this is a hell of a long way from London.'

Caroline finished her coffee. He showed her upstairs. The back room was thickly carpeted and the bed was made up in cosy warm colours.

'There is a spare toothbrush somewhere,' he said, rummaging about in the bathroom and emerging with a blue toothbrush still in its wrapping. 'And I can find you something to wear.'

Caroline followed him into the other bedroom. It was strange. The last man she had been in a bedroom with was Michael. She

181

was beginning to feel very sorry for herself. He emerged from the chest of drawers with a pretty blue nightdress.

'Will this do?'

'It's fine, thank you.'

'I'm sorry about this, I wasn't thinking. There is a key in the door if you want to lock it.'

He smiled slightly and wished her good-night and Caroline retreated into the back bedroom. It was a double bed. The curtains were not closed and it was cool. The snow had stopped. Outside was a view of a fell like a white sea. She heard him moving about next door for a while and then there was silence and she thought, 'How strange. People will think I've gone to bed with him.'

Village people, if they noticed, would talk. Men were completely gone from her personal life, the only time she met them was at work. It was odd how safe she felt. If they were burgled she wouldn't have to get out of bed. Not only was it not her house, but he was there. And in the morning, if her car wouldn't start or had a flat tyre, she felt sure he was the kind of man who could change tyres and recharge flat batteries.

It was funny, she thought as she got into bed, how men assumed that widows were desperate for sex when in fact what they were really desperate for was affection. It would have been nice to cuddle Stephen West, but even though he was by far the most attractive man she had met since Michael, she didn't want to have sex with him. She wanted Michael, nobody else would do.

The bed was comfortable. She had put out the light and pushed back the curtains. It snowed a little, not much, just light flurries like white fingers against the window. The bed soon warmed up. Feeling safer than she had felt in months, Caroline closed her eyes.

She awoke in the daylight and heard a soft knocking on the door. When she acknowledged it, Stephen opened the door and handed her a cup of tea.

'I'm digging your car out,' he said.

Caroline sat up to accept the tea and was rather disconcerted when he sat down on the bed.

'Did you imply that you don't like working for Gareth Forester?'

Caroline sat back against the pillows.

'I can't stand him,' she said frankly, 'but I need the money. In fact, I need more money.'

'You could help me. I'd be happy to accept

evenings and weekends if you like. I can't afford to pay anybody full-time just at present, but the office is in an awful state and I'll pay you as well as I can.'

'Fine,' Caroline said, and drank her tea.

Alex didn't understand why Matthew had telephoned and asked her to go to Gareth Forester's thirty-fifth birthday. It wasn't his style at all. In some obscure way, she thought he did it because of Andrew, because Andrew wouldn't be there, and if he had been then she would have been. She tried to plead work but he seemed to know that she was in Newcastle all that week and her social life was truly awful. She met lots of men and they all seemed to know that she was as good as widowed and they all wanted to go to bed with her and she did not want any of them, she did not trust them, they bored her, she disliked them.

She was, however, rather worried that she did actually want to go to a party with Matthew. For a start, he wouldn't try and grab her, but he would be there if she needed a safety net. She had not seen him since they had spent two days at the cottage and when he had left she had regretted his leaving and that was strange. It was like being treated to a private showing at a cinema, he was the person nobody else knew and he seemed to like being with her. She had no idea why, except that in some strange way he felt responsibility for her and no man had ever felt that except Andrew. How odd. They were not father and son but in some ways Matthew was like Andrew in that he cared and he didn't seem to want to get her into bed or put his hands on her.

She made herself look as good as she could manage. After all, there would be other men at the party and some of them would be single and she could have a good time. Sam would be there. She rather fancied him. There was nothing like confession for making you attracted to somebody, and Sam was kind and discreet and she even felt as though he liked her a little. But when she got there, he was busy, and Gareth Forester was all over her and she kept retreating from him. Matthew danced with Jess Beardsley and that was too difficult to watch, she felt so guilty about Jess, who looked like a lanky ghost. Alex felt so sorry for her, so sorry for what she had done. She tried to tell herself that Tom would have gone to somebody else if not her, but that didn't help. She had stolen Jess Beardsley's husband. However, if

Jess had known what a rat Tom really was, would she have grieved quite as much as she appeared to be doing?

Matthew danced several times with Jess but at the end he came back to Alex, so she didn't like to ask him anything.

'Let's drive to the cottage,' he said.

She didn't like to tell him that it was one in the morning and she was tired or that her house was only a few minutes away. She told him that it was a good idea, and it was, because she had him to herself there. She did not pretend to herself that she was not reliving the childhood she had not had. When they got there she ran up and down the freezing beach and he watched, laughing, only saying to her when she was tired out and her lips stung with salt, 'Come in. You must be exhausted.'

It was, she thought later, pathetic. How many times had her father not tucked her into bed and how many times had she wished he would? Matthew didn't do that, of course, but he did make hot chocolate for her and sit her by the fire. Alex thought she might never want to go back. They sat companionably there for a while and when she was about to go to sleep she took herself off to bed, only saying to him, 'Thanks for being there. I don't want to be embarrassing and I'm not trying to come on to you, but thanks.'

'I suppose it doesn't occur to you that I need you there too,' he said. 'And I'm not trying to come on to you either.'

'I want bacon sandwiches in the morning,' Alex said and she went off and fell into bed and slept the kind of sleep which adults claim children do and perhaps they don't, the soundest kind of sleep, where you can hear your parents' voices through the ceiling and know that if anything goes wrong they will take care of it. Matthew might never have been a parent, but as far as she was concerned it was a waste.

Twenty

For a few weeks after the party nothing changed. Jess went on as she had done, doors locked, watching television and taking the occasional walk on the beach and reading and then she got up one morning and she hadn't closed the bedroom curtains quite, there was a chink of light showing, and when she got up and pushed them back the sun poured into the room like somebody was letting it out of a bucket.

It was spring. She hadn't noticed. The sun was warm. It showed up the dust on the furniture. She decided to clean. At lunchtime she had forgotten to chill the wine, so it didn't taste as good as it should have, and she only managed two glasses. After that she decided to go for a walk on the beach. The tide was well down and there were dozens of pretty shells. A boy was running with his dog, a big black labrador. It was a very young animal and dashed up to her, leaped up and began to lick her face. The boy apologized but Jess only laughed and hugged it and watched it run back along the beach and into the water and out again. She began to think she might get a dog.

That evening she was bored. There was nothing on television and she had watched all her videos. She wanted to go out but there was nowhere to go, nobody she wanted to see. She wandered the flat, stood in front of the wardrobe. She had all Tom's clothes but somehow when she opened the wardrobe they didn't seem like his any more, they didn't smell like his, they smelled of her perfume somehow, perhaps her clothes had sort of wafted into them. They seemed to be hanging reproachfully.

She decided that she didn't need them to remind her of him. She and Tom had had what was almost a perfect marriage, she was not going to forget it. She could be rid of his clothes and somehow she felt that she would be better for it but it was not going to be easy. His suits were well tailored and she remembered him in them, how tall and elegant he had looked, how proud she had been to watch him go off in the mornings to work.

One by one she took out and folded his shirts, sweaters and trousers. The last thing she took down were his suits. The nearest charity shop would be pleased with all this. She had noticed a Red Cross shop in the high street, and she would feel as if she was doing some good.

The following day, she finished folding and packing the clothes and then she put them into big bags and drove the short distance to the shops, parking as close as she could.

When she explained that she had a lot of bags, the middle-aged women in the shop were helpful and two of them came to carry the bags. Jess lingered there. She liked it. The window had been carefully dressed in yellow and the shop was organized and interesting. Smiling women served behind the counter, thanked her profusely. Jess felt better, lighter. When she left the shop, she noticed that they were asking for volunteers, there was a paper in the window.

She went home and drank her coffee and watched the sea for a few minutes and then considered whether she ought to offer. She was too young, they wouldn't want her. She couldn't forget about it. The following day she went past it again and on the way back she gathered her courage and went inside. They seemed surprised but pleased at her offer and she went home happier than she had felt in a long time. She would be able to help, not to work properly, but it was a beginning, she would be able to talk to people, mix with them. She could go to the shop and sort clothes and iron and serve and be glad. She knew that other people would think it silly but she felt as if she had achieved something. It gave her purpose.

That evening, unable to go to the shop, she was also unable to be alone. The flat was so silent. She wanted to be with other people. She wished she could go somewhere. The next day was Sunday. The silence was finally oppressive. Jess picked up her purse and her car keys and fled. She got into her car and drove home.

It was a perfect spring day in the Tyne valley, quiet and green, and when she came out on the top before she turned left to go down into the village, it was a welcome, even though she was alone. She was glad to be there. She parked the car and walked in. It was probably the only house in the world that you could still just walk into. There was laughter coming from the sitting room and then she thought it was teatime and her Aunty Joan and Uncle Pete were there.

She was glad as soon as she went into the room. Her mother exclaimed excitedly and got up and kissed her. Her father tried to press tea on her. Her Aunty Joan kissed her as well, and her Uncle Pete told her she was the bonniest lass in the whole world, and it was to Jess as though some armour cracked, broke and fell off. She was glad to be there, she was pleased to be home. She drank tea and ate fruitcake and they made her laugh. Her Uncle Pete talked about his plans for the garden. Her mother and Aunty Joan discussed their neighbours and friends and slandered them freely, and her dad smiled at her from his armchair to the side of the fire.

Later her dad and Uncle Pete took her to the pub, where she was greatly admired by men who had known her since she was a little lass. She played darts and won. She drank beer and enjoyed it and then she walked home in the dark with her dad as she hadn't done in years. They asked her to stay and in the morning she could hear her mother and father talking in the kitchen and she turned over luxuriously in her bed and went back to sleep.

At half past ten she went down the stairs and her mother made bacon and eggs for her and a big pot of tea. She was in the shop that afternoon. She told her mother all about it and her mother seemed pleased, didn't urge her to stay, told her to keep in touch, kissed her and let her go. Jess sang on the way home.

After that Jess worked at the Red Cross shop twice a week. She was happy there. She had been completely accepted and got to know the other women. She soon got to the stage where she could say good morning to people on the street. She knew the shopkeepers, the old men who walked their dogs on the beach – she would greet their dogs by name and many would see her from far off and come bounding up to her.

She considered getting a dog but didn't. She would wait a while. She knew the children who lived nearby and those who came into the charity shop and, since she had a car, she was often sent to collect parcels of clothes and other goods.

One Sunday afternoon several weeks later, she was doing the window. It was the work she liked best. She had been given a free hand and, even if they didn't like her arrangements, the older women were too kind to say so since she obviously got such a lot out of doing it. This afternoon she was so engrossed that she had forgotten to lock the door. She turned swiftly from where she was arranging some books and said, 'We're

193

closed–' and then stopped. It was Matthew Elliot.

'Hello, Jess. I thought it was you.'

He must have eyes like a shithouse rat, Jess thought. How the hell could he have seen her from the road?

'Matthew.' Jess got out of the window, immediately aware of how she looked in her old dirty T-shirt and her grubby leggings. She had not thought after the party that he would contact her. He would not let her drive home but had not offered to take her home. He ordered her a taxi.

Rain had begun to fall. The big silver car shimmered under its sheen of water.

'What do you want?' she said.

'Nothing. I saw you against the glass.'

'You just happened to be driving up the main street?'

'No, I've been in Newcastle all week. I'm on my way home to London and I stopped to say hello to some friends who live here. Did you do last week's window?'

'You saw it?'

'It was very good, very striking. Want to come out and have a cup of tea?'

Jess was about to refuse automatically, men were always asking her out, looking at her. Workmen whistled in the streets, men

194

made excuses to come into the shop or approached her on the beach. She had heard every line in the book.

'All right,' she said. 'I'm finished.'

She almost offered to go home and change and then didn't. She locked the shop, they got into the car and he drove to the most expensive hotel in the area. In defiant mood, Jess didn't care how she looked. The car was whisked away, people grovelled, and very soon afterwards she was seated on a beautifully squashy sofa with a white tablecloth on a low table in front of her and a silver tea service.

Pink and white cakes oozed cream, sandwiches were perfect diamond shapes, cups and saucers were white, edged with gold, the cups so thin you could see your fingers through them. There was the gentle atmosphere of money, people spoke in soft voices, carpets dulled the sound of feet, and tables were placed at large intervals so that nobody should intrude on the conversation.

She watched him suspiciously as she watched all men now that she was alone. He was very careful. He didn't touch her, he didn't say anything which could have been interpreted as curious or condescending. He was, she thought, usually a man of few words, as though he had said everything he had to say and was rather tired, as if each word was a new sin or a luxury. Now he was throwing them out, being amusing, being interesting for her. He did it easily and she thought that perhaps only she would see it for an act.

He was not this insensitive. She suspected that he could be any kind of a bastard that he chose to be, but he was doing this so that she would not pick him up wrongly and accuse him of asking for anything more than another cup of tea, since the pot was near her.

He contented himself with sitting across from her drinking his tea. He didn't eat much. Jess had had no lunch and demolished half a dozen tiny sandwiches and a cream cake, licking her fingers in appreciation and drinking three cups of tea.

She began telling him about the shop, the people, the window and the women, and he seemed interested and then she said she ought to go. He didn't argue, he didn't try to make her have more tea or delay her. He drove her home and she got out of the car and he said goodbye.

The flat was so silent, Jess thought when she opened the door, the sound of his voice lingering in her mind. If he had asked to see her, if he had come after her, she would have resented it. As it was, suddenly she was without him and, for the first time since Tom's death, she wanted to spend time with another man.

She argued loudly with herself. Matthew Elliot was much too old, he must be ten years older than Tom had been. It was only then that she realized age had nothing to do with whether people liked and were attracted to one another. She missed him. She missed him even more the following day and the one after that. She got to the next Sunday. She spent all day making a mess of changing the window, hoping that he might suddenly appear, magicked because she wanted him to, but he didn't. She decided that she had done something wrong, that she should have dressed up, and then caught herself trying to be something for a man, a man she didn't know, a man her mother would have had a fit to think she was out with, a man her father didn't like and nobody in the village would have given house room to.

Matthew was a boss, a capitalist, he was the enemy. Tom had been successful, but not like this, and Tom had started out middle-class, so it didn't count, it was different. She determined to put him from her mind and then two weeks later, early one evening, he telephoned.

'I wondered...' She listened to him hesitating and smiled. 'I wondered,' he said again, 'if you would have dinner with me.'

All she had to say was no and she knew that would be it, she would never hear from him again. She just had to say the word.

'That would be nice,' she said and heard him let go of his breath.

'Is Saturday any good?'

Saturday was an eternity away, Jess thought, it was only Tuesday.

'That would be fine,' she said.

After she put down the telephone receiver, she changed her mind a hundred times. He would presume she was going to go to bed with him, men did. He was too old, she was too young, she couldn't tell anybody. She wouldn't be able to eat. She would drink too much. He had been out with lots of other women when he was married, he was not to be trusted, he was too clever for her. He had manipulated the situation, he had played her to here. That was when she realized she didn't have a telephone number for him even if she had wanted to ring and cancel.

She decided not to dress up. She wore her

plainest black dress. It looked incredible. It looked even better with the addition of a little jewellery. She wouldn't be able to think of anything to say. She didn't like him. He would be boring, he would try to put his hands all over her, it would be a disaster.

He was punctual. Jess was trembling so much that she almost didn't open the door and then she blamed him for putting her through all this. She invited him in. It was still light outside and he exclaimed over the view and started talking about the seabirds, not at all how she had envisaged it. She offered him a drink and he refused.

'Is it because you're driving?'

'I don't drink,' he said, frowning as some duck hit the water.

'What, never?'

'No.'

'Do you mind if other people do?'

'Certainly not. Look at that. You would think it had skis.'

Jess laughed as the little black and white birds skidded to meet the waves and he enthused about the flat and the view and it was so casual that she forgot to be nervous.

She had thought he would take her some-where very impressive in the city but they drove to a Chinese restaurant in the country and it was quiet there. The food was fun and they talked non-stop all evening. Jess listened to herself laughing and excused herself and went off to the ladies' room. There she saw herself transformed, sparkling eyes, glowing cheeks. She was ashamed. All she wanted was to go home.

She didn't have to tell him. Shortly afterwards they left. Nobody spoke during the thirty minutes or so it took to get back to the flat and they said goodnight and he left.

She was shaking when she got inside, closed the curtains in case the big silver car should still be there, but it wasn't, she checked five minutes later. She checked again five minutes after that, cursed him, cursed herself, reached for the wine and it had no taste, it didn't invite, didn't offer anything she could use. Neither did the television or the book she had thought so special – it had come from the Red Cross shop as did most of her books and even most of her clothes these days.

The following day at the shop, she was bored and kept looking out. She didn't want to talk to anybody, she decided that she hated ironing more than anything in the world. He didn't telephone, she had known that he wouldn't, but she didn't put the answering machine on and when people did ring she dived at it.

The days crawled past. The following weekend she spent the entire time by the telephone. A second week began and nothing happened. She cried several times. By the end of that week she was searching telephone books and ringing, trying to establish where he could be found, but apparently he had vanished, because there was no way he could be contacted. Presumably he hid behind other people in business, and in his personal life he gave his number only to people he wanted to have it.

On the Saturday evening, when she walked back from the shop, she could see the glint of the silver car a long way before she reached it.

There were dozens of silver cars, it wouldn't be his but, as she got nearer, it turned into a Mercedes and, as she got even nearer, he was leaning against the door, like somebody waiting for a bus or like a chauffeur who'd been told to hang about. He didn't look up when she reached him. Jess put her hands into her jeans pockets and leaned back beside him and waited.

'You telephoned me twice this week,' Matthew said.

'I just wanted to say something.'

'Which was?'

'I can't remember now.'

He took a card out of his pocket and offered it to her.

'You mean I can actually reach you on this number?' Jess said sarcastically.

'Day or night.' He opened the door as though he was going to get back into the car.

'Would you like to go for a walk?' Jess said.

Twenty-One

Alex had not been able to go back to the cottage without Matthew, he had ruined it for her. She had enjoyed those days of being alone before he arrived, but when she tried going back there in the spring she was restless and took no pleasure from it. She thought back over the years with Andrew and of what Matthew had been like then, the dreadful house in London where Margaret had presided and how he had rarely been at home, the scandals with other women in the tabloids.

She could no longer think of him in the same light. Her most enduring memory was of him lying asleep on the sofa and other images of him at the cottage, walking along the beach, laughing at something she had said, building up the fire in the sitting room, and she wished that she had not gone there.

She missed Tom's lightness. Being with him had been like a party, and yet she knew when she was being honest with herself that the affair had been over. Andrew had adored her. Nobody adored her now.

She worked very hard. She also tried to go to bed with other men but she couldn't. She couldn't touch anybody, she didn't want them. The only person she wanted to be around was Matthew. Fifty times or more she picked up the telephone and put it back down again.

Worse was to follow. She found out over the radio that the company she worked for had been taken over by another. Shortly after that her boss rang and fired her.

That evening Matthew turned up on her doorstep. Alex cursed herself. She had taken off her make-up, put on an old dressing gown, tied her hair back because it was in the way. She did not want to appear upset or vulnerable in front of somebody so successful.

'I heard,' he said.

Alex let him in, tried to think of an excuse to leave him alone in the sitting room while she made herself look human and couldn't think of one.

'I don't need any favours,' she said before he could go on. 'We are not related, even if you insist on pretending. You are nothing to me and I am nothing to you and it would be easier–'

'We have a vacancy in Newcastle,' Matthew said. 'Stop being so bloody noble and take it.'

'Matthew, I can't.'

'Yes, you can.'

'You don't know that I'm any good.'

'I have instincts about these things. Come on, Alex, say you will.'

Afterwards, when he had gone and she had slept, she heard his voice almost like a chant in her dreams. 'Come on, Alex, say you will.' She held the words to her like a hot-water bottle.

Twenty-Two

The pit was called the Sunny Mary. Caroline thought it was a wonderful name. She ran it around her tongue. Stephen's office was a disaster and there was nothing up there but the pit and the buildings, the fell, birds and sheep. She spent three weekends sorting out his filing system and the desks and the mess, and she went there every evening after work. The office was warm, there was an old-fashioned stove which ran on coal, so of course it was always kept very hot in the cool weather, banked down when the weather improved, so that you could boil a kettle on top of it.

On Saturdays and Sundays Stephen would be there, and in the evenings he never went home before half past seven, so she could finish her daytime job, go on up to the pit and find him there. He always had the kettle boiling for tea and she would bring sandwiches and cakes and she liked it there in the quietness, just the two of them. He went back to his parents' house when he left the pit. The men were long gone by six and he and Caroline sat around and drank tea by the stove and sometimes she didn't want to go home. He didn't have a separate office – when he was there he would sit with his feet up on the desk and they would work and it was companionable. He wrote letters and made telephone calls and took notes from files.

The summer had its good moments, its sunshiny days, but it didn't make much difference to Stephen. Mining was one job which went on regardless of the weather. It didn't matter what happened above ground. The mine had become, strangely, a place of refuge. There were no interruptions, there were no changes, everything went on just as always. There were problems but he knew most of them, having lived with mining as a child. He had reliable men, they knew how to work underground, they understood and lived with the dangers. They had seen accidents, death, illnesses. For generations people had taken coal from this land. Nothing new could go wrong.

Stephen spent more and more time with his father when he was not at work, so in the end he and Susan gave up the cottage. He hadn't wanted to. The distance between himself and his parents was like the last place of safety, but she seemed to hate it more and more as the weeks went by.

They fought about it as they fought about most things, and when she tried to hit him he got hold of her, tight fingers around her arm, and he shouted at her. He was aware that it hurt but it didn't stop him. He was only just stopping himself from knocking her across the room. The temper shot through him like molten steel and was only just below the surface. Another insult, another word, and she was going to be sorry in a way in which she had not been before.

His head went crazy, like it was blowing up, and for the first time ever he understood why men hit women, the frustration, the long slow drip of sustained responsibility unchained the red-hot feeling which would only be eased by lashing out. And then the moment passed. He looked down at the offending fingers but they didn't move and he couldn't unclasp them. She had gone pale. Her eyes were full of tears and something else which he hadn't seen before. She was afraid.

Very slowly the fingers unfastened but the damage was done. Her face twisted and the tears began to drop like rain.

'I'm sorry,' he said as she ran out of the room. He went after her but she went upstairs and locked herself in the bedroom and, however much he apologized from beyond the door, she would not listen. He didn't blame her.

Since they had moved back, his mother always seemed to take Susan's side over everything and he had no doubt that she would later go off to the kitchen, where his mother had been busy lately harvesting the garden, making tomato chutney and raspberry jam and she would tell his mother everything.

Stephen went to work. That day there was an accident, not a bad one, but a man was hurt. It was the youngest Elliot brother, John. Stephen took him to hospital and when he came back at the end of the afternoon his hands shook so much that he could barely drive. He went into the office.

'John all right?' Caroline said.

'Fine. I drove him home.' Stephen sat down at his desk and a weariness came over him.

'Would you like tea?' Her voice sounded anxious. He nodded and smiled. She made the tea, poured it, put the mug on the desk, but Stephen couldn't pick it up.

'Don't you want it?'

'I need a drink.'

'Shall I take you to the pub?'

'Victoria will be home by now, won't she?'

'She's never there,' Caroline said. 'She's going to a party tonight. She'll spend two hours getting ready. She's considering a nose stud, you know. It'll be tattoos next. I could take you to the Cross Keys for a swift drink and then run you home.'

'I said I'm all right.' He glared at her. Caroline looked coolly back at him.

'I know. That's what I kept telling people after Michael died. Like being cut in half. You don't feel anything, because the wound is too deep. It doesn't heal, you just go on being half.'

The Cross Keys was not a workman's pub, it was quite a stylish place. Stephen had a wash before they went, it was the best he could manage, but they knew him in there anyway so it didn't matter. He had gone there with his father from an early age. Going in with Caroline and sitting up to the bar was easy. It was a wet night and the fire was on, and Caroline drank beer with him and they ate crisps and then had a plate of chips each with mayonnaise. Other people came and went and talked to them and the landlord, since it was early on a midweek evening, hadn't much to do and he stood, polishing glasses and joining in the conversation, and he made beef sandwiches for them.

Halfway through the evening Caroline protested that she must start drinking orange juice because she was driving, but Stephen persuaded her to stay. She made him laugh, she made him forget about the business failing and his father dying and his wife sulking at home. They lingered over coffee and biscuits and she seemed pleased with his company. They were sitting on the sofa by the fire and he fell asleep for a few moments against her.

'Sorry,' he said, sitting up.

'You should go back to London,' Caroline said. 'You weren't meant for this.'

He knew that well enough. He longed for the city now, the noise, the excitement and the look and feel of words on paper. It was a growing hunger.

'Do you miss Frankfurt?'

'Every moment. Quite often when I wake up I have a few moments when I think I'm still there and everything is all right.'

She didn't go on. Nobody said anything

for a long time and it was comfortable. She fell asleep. He felt her gradually relax. When he was sure that she was sound, he eased her aside and then picked her up and carried her upstairs. It wasn't far and the stairs were wide and easy and she was small. She was getting thinner and thinner. Didn't anybody care about her? She was so light in his arms, much smaller than Susan, and yet she faced him as an equal and asked for nothing but her pay. Soon she wouldn't even have that, the way the business was going.

He pushed open the bedroom door and put her down carefully and in her sleep she made a little noise of protest as he drew away, so in the end he gave the door a shove and lay down and she folded herself in against him with another sigh.

Stephen felt free for the first time in many months. Nobody wanted anything. He didn't have to stay there, he had asked for two rooms but he was full of beer and chips and beef and the memory of an evening of laughter and good conversation. She slept on.

When Caroline awoke he was lying there looking at her, the beautiful soft brown eyes intent. After a moment or two he leaned over and kissed her. She could taste and smell coal. It was redolent of childhood, the closeness of other people, of something long since lost, like the cries of children playing in the wet garden when the air was sharp and stars were about to shine, bodies close in the game, hidden, hardly breathing, the sky dotted here and there with lighted windows, and the secrecy and quietness of not being found.

Very slowly, nothing but his mouth and the deceit and being there in the silence of the new day not quite begun, night paling beyond the window. And then his fingers in among her clothing, deft, and she closing her eyes for the palms of his hands on her, and then reaching up and bringing him nearer so that she could taste and feel him better, the kisses deeper and her hands full of his shirt.

'Stephen...'

He didn't hear her the first time, so she said his name again and found herself looking into his eyes, glinting brown lights like gems.

'What?' he said softly.

'Nothing, just...'

It was not that she didn't want him. She had even lately looked at Gareth Forester and

213

wondered what he was like and that, she thought, was desperation. Stephen was the right man, he was partly hers, in the office where his wife had no place, and of late they had spent a great deal of time together. She felt good with him, she always did, it didn't matter what was happening. The trouble was that he was married and she felt married but that didn't stop her and it didn't make her stop him, but she knew very well that nothing altered things quite so much as having sex with a man, it told you so much about him.

He hadn't had sex much lately, she could tell that, even though he was careful and slow. He wasn't getting on with his wife but she hadn't known it had got as far as the bedroom. Also, there was an edge. He was on the verge of bankruptcy, grieving over his father, and lately he had told her that he thought the house would have to be sold. That kind of thing was like being a fox on the run. It sharpened your survival instincts.

'You all right?' she said.

'Mm.'

'You sure?'

'Oh yes.'

He smiled against her ear. Funnily, the best part of it was just that he was there, that was what she missed, having somebody who thought she mattered in that way, not being ignored, not being left alone. She liked him, it was not a desperate act with a stranger, it was in fact like having Michael, and that alone made it worthwhile.

For this time, if no other, she could have the illusion of his being alive, of his love and affection for her, because Stephen West was not the kind of man who could perform such an act anonymously, though she was sure that some men might.

He was both himself and Michael and, if he knew it, which she thought he might, he didn't seem to mind. She liked the way that they were so easy together and she could put her fingers into his hair and slide her hands down his body in reassurance that no one had died.

She liked the way that he cradled her in his arms so that nobody could hurt her, it deflected so many of the problems over the past months and she really was very pleased that the aching in her body eased, ceased and in its place he provided pleasure. It was like eating a whole tub of ice cream or drinking a chilled bottle of champagne all to yourself on a hot afternoon. He was chocolate fudge cake and lemon pudding and crème caramel.

Stephen had gone to see Sam, he didn't know who else to talk to about the pit, and Sam was the one person he knew who would be constructive, who would not criticize.

'I've had an offer for the pit. Matthew Elliot wants to buy it.'

'What on earth for?' Sam asked, unable to contain his surprise.

'I don't know. I would keep it going if I could, but we have no money, we can't get the coal out cheaply enough to pay the men, and the equipment necessary is more than I can afford. On the other hand...'

'On the other hand?'

'My parents don't like him. I know it sounds stupid, Sam–'

'No, no,' Sam said calmly.

'If they won't sell, what am I going to do? If I don't sell, we're going to lose everything.'

'Can you explain that to them?'

'I might if you were there. Would you do that?'

'Certainly, if you think it'll help. What did he say?'

'He said that if I was considering selling or closing he would be interested in buying.'

'I could ring him, make it official, if you

like. I do a lot of his legal work.'

'Thanks, Sam, that would be great.'

Sam couldn't imagine why Matthew Elliot would want the Sunny Mary. It was not a venture which made money and it would take a great deal of investment to make it even possibly viable, and even then it could lose. Would he close it out of some kind of revenge? He was difficult to contact. Sam tried ringing and leaving messages and was therefore surprised when four days later Matthew turned up at the office without an appointment. It was unlike him to do so.

'I was in the area and I got your message,' he explained when Sam apologized for keeping him waiting.

Sam offered him a seat, looked at him and saw a change. The closed look had gone from his eyes. It was not an obvious thing, he doubted anybody else would notice and, if Matthew was happy, it didn't show, but then neither had grief nor unhappiness. He hid his feelings well but it was just as though somebody had lifted a veil off his eyes. They were not as dark as usual.

'It's about the Sunny Mary,' Sam said. 'Stephen West said that you had indicated you might be interested in buying if he was interested in selling.'

'I take it he is.'

'If the offer was right.'

'He's going down the sink,' Matthew said flatly.

'If the Sunny Mary goes, it will take the village with it. Is that too much for your stomach?'

Matthew laughed.

'You mean the golden memories of my childhood? Matthew Elliot, saviour of Burnside?'

'The only other motive I can think of is that you want to see it close.'

'If I wanted that, I don't have to buy it,' Matthew pointed out. 'There was a time when I would have enjoyed watching the Wests lose their living and their house, but the old man's dying and the old lady ... revenge has to have flavour to be any good. I'm interested. I'd like to see if it could be made to work.' He named a price. 'Tell Stephen he ought to make his mind up soon. When Ted West dies, it'll take a lot more sorting out.'

'Do you think it could be made profitable?' Sam asked and he had to make himself meet Matthew's arctic-blue gaze.

'That's the interesting part,' Matthew said.

'Older people can be stubborn.'

'Oh, I'm sure you can persuade almost anybody to do anything,' Matthew said. 'Ring me when you've sorted it.'

Sam stared at the door for quite a long time after Matthew had gone. He didn't understand what was happening here or quite why Matthew didn't like the Wests. They had done no more to him than to anybody else, as far as he knew, less in fact, since Matthew had got out of Burnside when he was about seventeen, by all accounts. And if he really had disliked them, then surely he would have enjoyed seeing the pit close. He had not been back there for twenty years, as far as Sam knew, and it was hardly his usual line of work. What could Matthew possibly know about coal mining?

Sam would go ahead and talk to the Wests and try to persuade them to sell, but it was for Stephen that he would do it. If Mr West died, Mrs West would inherit everything and she was the kind of person who was not prepared to acknowledge her husband could have done anything wrong, so how much more would she cling to this idea once he was dead? Stephen would lose everything. Sam only wished he could have found a buyer whom the Wests liked or respected

219

enough for them to consider the offer dispassionately. He doubted they could be made to see that they had no alternative.

The following afternoon when Stephen was in the pit office, Philip Elliot burst in.

'Is this true about our Matt trying to buy the pit?'

Stephen didn't know what to say. Nobody knew except himself and Sam and Sam was so close-mouthed he was legendary for it.

'Where did you hear that?'

'Never mind where I heard it,' Philip said, sounding rather like his brother, 'is it true?'

While Stephen searched for an answer, Philip answered himself.

'It bloody is!' he said and stormed out.

'We can't keep it from my parents,' Stephen told Sam when Sam arrived that evening, the time they had planned to talk it over with his mother and father. 'Everybody knows.'

'I can't think how.'

'He's not exactly inconspicuous and he has been spending an awful lot of time around here just lately.'

'Why is that?'

'I don't know. I thought you would, you

know everything.'

It was as Stephen had predicted. His father became agitated and his mother said outright that it was out of the question that they should ever sell the pit and that to sell to a man like that – they would not do it, not even to someone of good moral character, but Matthew Elliot...

'You're upsetting my husband,' Mrs West said and opened the door of the room. 'Young men, they know nothing.'

She accused Stephen of being incompetent when they got as far as the kitchen, and told Sam that she was only glad his father wasn't there to see what he was doing and what kind of man he had turned out to be. She said she was not surprised that his wife had left him, she was not surprised that Susan cried all the time, because Stephen was the kind of man who rarely came home and when he did he was drunk and he had hit her. She had seen the evidence. They were a pair of no-good meddling fools.

'Christ, I'm sorry,' Stephen apologized when they finally got to the door and his mother closed it after them. They walked down the drive in silence. 'Is there anything more we can do?'

'Not unless you want to forge their

signatures, and I wouldn't advise it.'

'I wonder how people found out.'

The following morning Sam asked Kathleen to come into the office and close the door.

'Did you tell somebody what went on between Matthew Elliot and me in here yesterday?' he said softly.

'No.'

'It was all over the village by the afternoon and nobody else knew. You know that what goes on in here is confidential.'

'I've never told anybody anything,' she said.

'Until yesterday.'

'It wasn't me, it was Sandra from the bank. We saw him outside getting in the car and that young woman was there and she said something about buying and selling and the pit. It wasn't in here, it was outside. That big flash car of his was parked on the hill where it wasn't meant to be parked and she was waiting for him and she looked all anxious and I was just going out for my break with Sandra and we heard it.'

'And you thought that made it all right?'

'I didn't say anything and I could hardly stop Sandra. It would matter to that lass, wouldn't it, her dad working for them and her coming from there.'

'Who?'

'That lass whose husband died, that Jess Beardsley,' Kathleen said. 'If Matthew Elliot wanted to keep it quiet, he wasn't making a very good job of it,' and she went out and slammed the door after her.

Twenty-Three

To Matthew, Jess was a new beginning, not like other beginnings, not like other women, not like a business or a dawn or a new year, it was like falling in love at sixteen for the very first time, when everything was more in touch with everything else. And it was strange because at least to begin with his relationship with Jess was not a physical thing. She didn't want to be near him.

He didn't blame her for that and he could see that what she needed was somebody to look after her, to be there, to fill the places where Tom had been which he no longer filled, and they were to do with her loneliness and that huge gap between Tom's death and here. It had nothing whatsoever to do with lips and hands and bodies, it was freezing-cold shock and a sickness and a horrible fatality which needed to be erased and somehow for some reason only he could do it.

There were dozens, hundreds of men who would have been glad to take care of Jess, but she would let no one close in any way except him. She tolerated general conversation, she was happy to talk to people in the street or on the beach, but nobody was asked to the flat, not even her parents, it seemed as though the very touch of another person might burn her, hurt her further, and no further hurt could be endured, he had seen that.

She let him into her flat, where he was careful until he realized that he could be happy just knowing she would allow him there. He liked to watch the birds on the shoreline, especially when the tide was up. It was then as though the ducks were partying, the gulls gathered, no doubt to feed, and the curlews with their wonderful beaks lined up along the shore like people at a long, wide bus stop. The sand under them was shiny and wet like cement, and the sea beyond them broken, as the weather warmed and Jess warmed too.

They went out together, not where other people might be, just generally. They walked on the beach, she liked that best, they went to the shops nearby and in the evenings they sat out on the balcony of her flat, wearing sweaters, since the summer was almost non-existent, and she would drink wine and he would drink tea. She wasn't getting through half as much alcohol as before, as far as he could judge, and it was easy to tell how upset she was by how much she drank. By July she was rarely drinking during the day and, if he could distract her sufficiently, it took her the entire evening to get through less than a bottle of wine.

It reminded him uncomfortably of his childhood, but then his mother and father had been drunks of a different calibre and had ruined their lives and the early lives of their children with their despair and destruction, whereas all Jess had seemed to want to destroy was herself. That was almost gone.

He was away a lot but she didn't seem to mind and he thought that Tom had been away a great deal and she could slip back into the old ways, at least to some extent. He could be Tom, coming and going. When he was away he telephoned her constantly and he could hear by the lightness in her voice that she was all right. She went to the Red Cross shop almost every day and she hung on to that, she seemed to gain so much from helping.

She saw her parents. Matthew was aware that she had not told them about him and he knew very well that they would disapprove and that she could not bear their disapproval. She could not have borne much more, he could tell when he met her. She was on the very brink of life. She told him that she thought she had died and not Tom because there could not be so much pain in the world as people had to bear, therefore she must be dead.

Matthew thought he understood that loneliness, he had felt to some extent the same kind of thing for twenty years. After Margaret died – she had been ill for two years – he felt so guilty. He had been brought up in a culture where someone was to blame for everything. They had known one another all their lives, so he felt that it was not just the man he had become who she was leaving, but the boy that he had been.

To have to marry was a disgrace which was soon forgotten. They would have lived in the same street or the next street to where their parents lived, except that Margaret could not stay near her parents. Men worked, women made a home and had children. The land, the pits, the docks were the traditional work in the north-east for men like him, but his family were not pleased when he started working on the local markets, his mother thought he should go into the Co-op or an

227

office as a clerk and was unhappy when he refused. From the beginning, he kept his family well and it was an embarrassment.

'Where did you get all this money?' Margaret would say, as though in fear that he had stolen it.

She didn't like it that they had more than other people, or the way that he would buy her presents. Men didn't do things like that. They tipped up their wages, were given pocket money, they went to the pub, they talked about their work and their money was hard come by, because they had sweated for it in somebody's foundry or shipyard or down another man's mine, but Matthew didn't have to sweat to make money. It came as naturally to him as breathing and it was fun. She was ashamed of him. In those days he could talk anybody into buying anything, it was a game, but working the markets was not a respectable way to make money, not to his family.

'That's how the Jew boys go on,' his mother said.

He had soon become rich enough to take Margaret away from the north-east, something he had longed to do, but she felt as though she was not good enough, she had no place. She could not break through into middle-class respectability. Now he understood her reluctance. At the time it only seemed that she was deliberately holding him back.

Not that he admired the middle classes, clinging to their respectability like a man holding on to a cliff edge in a thunderstorm, people who regarded their homes like precious jewels, men who feared women and women who feared one another and who bowed to the god of money as though it would buy them a place in heaven, Perhaps they had nothing to hope for. But he was soon beyond them and into the kind of new upper class where bright people could achieve anything.

Margaret had made no secret of the fact that she hated the life he had built for them. Her cooking was as bad as their marriage, so meals were not something to look forward to and it was always so formal, you couldn't lounge over a curry, you had to sit up to the table and eat properly, vegetables boiled until they wilted, potatoes without butter, beef cooked until it shredded.

She wore hideous dresses in camel and fawn and sludge green, vile and expensive. Her conversation was about people they had known when they lived in Burnside, she kept in touch, sometimes she went back, but he was not invited either to his own parents' or her mother's. She told him about his brothers and their families until he began to eat out and come home late and then he did not see Andrew before Andrew went to bed.

He was not allowed into her bedroom, she turned the key in the lock every night. They had a big row – he could not remember what it was about, how silly – but it had seemed so important at the time and she had left their bedroom and was never in it again, she told him that he was too tired to make love and that she would rather be alone if he couldn't do any better. It was true, he was always exhausted, but in time he found enough energy to make love to less exacting women. He had not worked out whether money and status made up for everything.

Each summer she would go home for the entire school holidays and take Andrew with her, which was where Andrew's love of the north had come from, he knew. She didn't want to go anywhere else. He came to understand how people's marriages fell apart. It was not an instant thing and once you had gone through it you couldn't see back, it was like a tunnel closing in behind you all the time, as though something had fallen and blocked the end.

There was nothing but darkness behind and you could not tell the difference between what you had done wrong and right and what she had done and there were always so many grievances which had to be called to account during the next row. He was too tired for rows. Not going home was much simpler and as he became prosperous there were always available women and some of them were so beautiful it hurt your eyes, and to his amused dismay he had turned into the kind of man who liked women who agreed with him, who would undress for him and make all the right noises.

Andrew had never been his son in any way, had never liked him, and he missed the son who had not liked him. He remembered Andrew being a little boy, afraid of the waves on the seashore and the lions in the bedroom. Some people, having lost their children to the teenage years, managed to get them back as they grew older, but he hadn't had that with Andrew. He thought of the few times he had ever gone upstairs to read a bedtime story and had invariably fallen asleep on the bed.

Andrew had been afraid of the sea, afraid of the dark, he had thought that lions were coming to get him in his bedroom. Matthew had found a poster with lions on it and taken the poster into the bedroom, taken Andrew by the hand and together they had brought the poster down the stairs and fastened it with drawing pins on the kitchen wall and after that the lions were tamed and never went into Andrew's bedroom again.

Jess had been working-class and middle-class, rich and poor, and it seemed to him that she had cared for none of it, that was what he liked about her. All she had wanted was for Tom to come home to her at the end of the day and for there to be a meal and a fire and a bottle of wine.

Matthew struggled to get back to her, cancelled any number of important meetings, spent a great deal of time in Newcastle, to the detriment of everything else. Each evening when he could not reach her became a failure and, when he got to her, there was always dinner and there was the warmth of her greeting, the relief on her pretty smiling face. What more could a man ask than to have a woman treat him like that? There was nothing and he knew it. All the women he had tried to love had not meant a quarter of what Jess meant now, and if he was Tom to her and not himself, he didn't really mind except that it turned out not to be like that.

One night that summer – late, it was June and in the north it was a perfect evening such as you sometimes got – the tide so far down beyond the rocks that you had to squint to see the barely breaking waves, the sun lingering in the pale sky and a stillness on the seashore which was the finest sound in the world. He had come back tired, he had driven a long way that day, refusing Oswald's help – his driver who lived in London and had got old. Matthew couldn't turn him out – he drove 300 miles to get to her and when he got there the windows were open to the evening quiet, she was wearing a long thin sleeveless yellow dress which she had probably got from the Red Cross shop, haute couture it was not.

The table was set and the candles were just lit and through the open window he could hear the sound of the gulls in the clear air. She hadn't heard him and when he walked into the sitting room she gave a sweet cry of surprise and launched herself off the sofa and ran, eyes lit like dark jewels, her arms coming up around his neck. She kissed him.

'I have waited and waited for you.'

'I know. I'm sorry I'm late. The A1 is the world's stupidest road and every idiot in creation was on it.'

She didn't let go. He hadn't expected that. He had expected chatter, a nice dinner, good wine, but not that she should let herself stay in his arms. She kissed him again, she put herself against him and her mouth was soft and warm and lingering.

He had hoped for this, dreaded it, imagined that he would turn into Tom – or not and either way it would be disastrous – and that she would turn into any one of a dozen women he had not loved and hoped to, but it wasn't like that one little bit.

She trusted him and it could have been that she trusted him not to be Tom, or it could have been just timing, or it could have been that the world was a better place than it used to be, or that God had decided at last to give him a break that way. Whatever, the love lasted beyond the obvious and he was so relieved.

He did not have to wish he hadn't done it, he didn't have to go home afterwards to Margaret and the hideous mess she had made of the house which he had once cared for, and to her disapproval, which was never spoken, and her tight thin lips. It was all gone except for Jess, who put on some white robe and she looked like an angel, except that she threw herself at him, laughing.

Her shoulders were so kissable and her eyes were stars and he knew in those seconds that he would never be able to leave her. He wanted to ask her to marry him right then and, since he could not, he contented himself with kissing her and being glad, and there was a cynical middle-aged part of him which said that he must etch upon his mind these moments with her, because, whatever else he had learned, he knew that you must consign very carefully to memory each dear moment. The happiness would be paid for again and again and the price was always huge, was always unexpected.

He had an image of God sitting some-where thinking up new ways of payment, unexpected horrors. Perhaps it was not so, perhaps the balance was uneven and he and Jess had already paid for this. She certainly looked as though she had. The pain in her eyes was never quite gone, even now, in his arms where she had nothing to fear and nobody to look for, it was still there. Who could acknowledge such things and be easy? He had learned to live without love. This was like having the door open and the fire lit and the easy chairs around the fire and a family such as no one had ever known. If he could hold the illusion, he would not ask for anything else.

Jess hadn't told her mother, she hadn't realized that everybody knew, or at least her parents and the people in the village. Her mother was shocked, Jess had known she would be. Why couldn't they let her get on with what was left of her life? She couldn't tell her mother that Matthew Elliot was the only thing which was keeping her sane, the only person she could trust not to hurt her. She didn't know why, her mother seemed to think he was bad for her.

'Do you know how many women he's had? You're just another one to him. He was married all those years and he was unfaithful to Margaret all the time. Where do you think that leaves you?'

Jess could remember Frankfurt in the early morning, the sound of cars on the road so far below. She could remember turning over in bed and her husband's back, his shoulders. Sometimes, if she thought hard late at night after a bottle of wine, she could remember what his laughter sounded like, what his body looked like when he was dressed in a particular suit. She remembered his face and his arms and his blue shirt and how she had been able to turn over and have him there. She could remember the nightmares and how he was there in the darkness and how she knew that he always would be.

The other night she had turned in the darkness and Matthew was there. He was a light sleeper. Tom had been a heavy sleeper, sometimes he had snored, but every time she awoke, Matthew was either awake or would awaken immediately. In his arms in the darkness, she could almost remember what happiness was.

'You don't need his money,' her mother said harshly, 'and you know that you can come home. I don't understand you.'

As though the lack of understanding was Jess's fault somehow, as though Matthew could do her any harm. There was nothing left to harm. Sometimes she thought she could put her hands through walls, ghost-like.

'People don't like him. They won't tolerate him buying the pit, you know.'

She went to the window that evening when she got back to the flat. It was a full summer sea, high and breaking gently on the shore. The sun was beginning to sink.

Matthew would come home to her. Her mother had talked on and on about him and about her and about the pit and the village people and about how faithless and ruthless and evil he was. Her voice had risen and fallen, louder and louder.

'People get over things, you know,' she had said. 'Life goes on. During the war, women's husbands died every day, it was so common and nobody took any notice. They got on with their lives, a lot of them married again. They didn't run around having affairs with men like Matt Elliot.'

That was only, Jess thought, because they couldn't. No woman in her right mind would refuse Matthew. He didn't moan, he didn't argue. He telephoned when he said he would, he was as punctual as he could be, considering his work, he didn't make stupid conversation or have moods, he wasn't difficult and he wasn't afraid of women, he didn't fear competition like many men.

He was generous and kind, he was complimentary about food and he was interested in what she was doing. He liked to watch the seabirds from the window. And he was very nice in bed, no insecurities, no pushy maleness, and during the night terrors he was there. All she wanted was for him to come home and then to be in his arms.

'People know,' she said, 'and they know about you buying the pit as well.'

'I'm not buying it any more. Old Man West won't sell.'

'Why not?'

'He doesn't like me.'

'I like you,' Jess said.

'I like you too.'

Twenty-Four

Caroline couldn't believe what she had done. When each of them calmly went off to work – she was very late, but for once nobody said anything. She muttered something about being worried about her mother. She was telling lies. How awful, but what else could she say? She sat in front of her desk all that afternoon and worried and called herself names and couldn't believe how stupidly she had behaved. She went to the pit in the evening and everything was normal, just as it had been. There he was, sitting on the desk, talking on the telephone, only pausing to say, 'Caro, have you got the Campbell file?' just as though nothing had happened. He talked on the telephone for the better part of an hour, he wrote rapidly for the following hour and when the telephone rang at half past seven and it was his wife, Caroline barely knew what to say. Susan West did not acknowledge her. She said, 'Can I talk to my husband, please?' So Caroline handed over the receiver and listened to him making short, non-commit-tal replies. That wasn't different, he always did that.

Caroline made some tea. Up to a week ago they had had tea when she got there, but lately things had been complicated and the closed expression on his face told her that it would not be long before the pit shut for good. There was something completely desperate about him now. He was there because he had to be there and that was all. He went home because he had to go home.

'Stephen...' she managed just before nine, and he looked up straight away, as though he had been waiting for her to say some-thing. 'Tell me it was a mistake.'

He got up and came to her and then he pulled her up out of her seat and kissed her.

'It was a mistake,' he said and then he kissed her again. It was just as good as it had been that morning, in fact, if anything could be better, it was. She couldn't think how to refuse. She had been married to Michael for such a long time that questions of this kind didn't occur. He had belonged to her and she to him. This man didn't belong to her but that wasn't how it felt. He was intent on kissing as much of her as he could reach and his hands were already under her sweater.

She made herself not kiss him, move back, but it took all the strength she had, the desk solid behind her and his body in front like a trap.

He would have moved closer but she said, 'No,' and put up both hands in defence.

'So, it was a mistake?'

'Yes.'

He backed off, he did it completely.

'I'm sorry,' Caroline said, 'I wish it had been different.'

'That I was Michael,' he said roughly.

'I should go home.'

She went. He didn't say a word, not even goodnight. Caroline ran towards the car. She wanted Michael so badly that she was crying when she got there. It seemed to her that she could feel and taste him on Stephen West, or was it the lack of him? She was wondering whether to drive and cry at the same time, when the driver's side door opened and he got in beside her.

'I didn't mean to make you cry. I'm so bloody angry with myself. I shouldn't have done it. Susan isn't to blame for any of this. It was my idea to give up my job and move north. It isn't her fault and I've behaved so badly, but I just ... I want to blame my father for dying, but I can't do that either.'

Caroline managed to halt the tears.

'It was so nice,' she said.

'It was, wasn't it?' He looked conspiratorially at her and grinned.

'I have to go.'

'It was only once. It won't happen again. Don't cry any more, OK?'

'All right,' Caroline said.

Even then he got hold of her and kissed her all over her face as though, because he didn't kiss her lips, it wasn't somehow official, and then he let her go.

Sam had never before cursed his ability to read other people, but he did so over the affair between Caroline and Stephen West. He knew that it was happening the day that it did, he was sure. Caroline's eyes looked like emeralds. It was almost as though Michael had come home. He understood that.

After Jo had left him, every time he met another woman, his body had signalled the chance for affection, and his mind had tried to relieve itself of loneliness. It was like fishing, and each time you cast the line thinking you would catch a salmon, only the trouble was you hadn't or you didn't know what you had caught, it certainly wasn't something you wanted to stay with.

How many times had he thought he was in love, only to find that the second time he saw someone, it was a disaster? Not the kind of disaster where important things happened, rather that nothing happened, that he could make nothing happen. One night in such circumstances, when he had muttered excuses, the girl had leaned across the table in the pub and said, 'I know just how you feel, love. All you want is to go home.'

To go home and shut the door. Oh, the relief of not having to take with you the person whose company you had sat through for the endless hours until you felt it was respectable to leave.

Caroline was different. He had not known she would be. If he had he would have done something about it, but it was too late, his timing was awful. She had gone to Stephen West. He would have tried to rescue her from that even if he hadn't thought he loved her. Stephen was married and Susan was not the kind of woman to give in, but he could understand why Caroline wanted Stephen. Stephen was glamorous. What a dreadful word, but it was true. He looked like a poet. Enough to make anybody shudder, but he did. He was blond and slender and his eyes were tragic.

Sam wanted to groan over that, but he couldn't, because he knew what it was like when your father died. Old Man West had been a cantankerous difficult bastard in his day, but he was still Stephen's father and Stephen, as an only child, had a close relationship with his parents. Sam understood that, because he had been as like an only child as it was possible to be, except that his parents had been easy people to get on with. He missed them both so much.

But he missed Caroline McIver as you could only miss a person whom you imagined loving and had not. He missed the time they had not had, the days they had not shared. He even missed the children they might have had. Sometimes Sam wondered what it would be like to have a child of your own but, even though he tried very hard, he never met anybody that he could think to have a child with after Jo had left him.

She had married again and now she had a baby and it hurt him. Dominic had been Sam's child. He knew somehow it was the closest he would get. When Dominic had died so had his hope. He didn't understand why. Older men than he was had children, but you could not, even from desperation, have a child with a woman you didn't love –

at least he couldn't.

He had met Jo at university and fallen in love with her the moment he saw her. The feeling had never happened again and he had begun to think that it was something to do with how old you were and how you felt when you had no more responsibility than lectures and parties and being loyal to your friends, that golden time when his parents had looked after Dominic – the best time of his life, when his father and mother were well, and running the practice.

He and Jo had lain in his narrow bed and all around them had been the claustro-phobic life of a small university town where you could walk down the street and see half a dozen people you knew, run up and down the beach drunkenly at three in the morn-ing, where you could take off your shoes, and screaming, dash under the sprinklers on the golf course, where life held promises, when you were young. How had it all gone so wrong?

And Caroline. He had not thought after all this time that he could love again. And it was stupid, he knew it was. Middle-aged love was not like young love, when you thought you would be together for life, have a child, grow old, remember together the first grandchild, the old days when you knew one another's parents. Couples like that had everything.

He knew he would never have it. He had grown used to the idea of being alone. People who were alone knew the silence, enjoyed the solitude, harnessed what they had, if they were sensible, and in some ways he had been lucky. He had money and a unique house and the trust of those who employed him, and he wanted very much to help them, to make their difficult lives better, simpler.

Lawyers, Sam thought, in these days, were more important than priests, or as important. Outside, there were lions. Within his office where the birds almost flew, he would shield people as God threw them, without thought, over the cliff edge. He had the awful feeling that he was falling over the cliff edge himself for the last time, and there would be no one to save him. Caroline was in love with Stephen West. Who was he to disillusion her?

A short time after this, when they had managed to keep a distance between them for so many days that Caroline lost count and began to think of it in weeks, she realized how much it meant to her to have Stephen at least partly hers, because there was nothing else.

There was work and, somewhere in the distance in the fog, there was her love for Michael and there was Victoria who had become an adult and barely needed her and had acquired a boyfriend called Graham who was almost always at the house, and there was her mother and living at her mother's house. She was grateful and her mother was kind, but she knew that her mother would have loved to have had the house to herself again and who could blame her for that? Caroline loved her the more for not complaining at all the problems they had brought her and all the small irritations of every day.

Getting up in the mornings had become almost impossible and working for Gareth Forester was never easy. And she thought it was funny but, when you get to that stage, when you think it can't get any worse, then it does and then it does it again and, just as you are about to drop off the end, things change.

She went into work one hot day that summer, she was early and there was nobody around but Sam. He was always first to arrive and last to leave. That particular day, Caroline didn't know why she had gone in early, it was bad enough being there the rest of the day, but she hadn't slept, she wanted to leave the house, so she was at least half an hour ahead of everyone, and Sam came into her office and he said, 'I'd like to have a word before the others arrive, if you've got a minute.'

Caroline was surprised but she nodded and followed him into his office. He asked her to sit down and then he said, 'Kathleen is leaving. I wondered whether you might consider coming to work for me. Do you think you might be interested?'

'Interested? Are you joking? I would love to work for you.'

'There's something else which goes with the job. The cottage.'

Caroline stared at him.

'What?'

'It's empty and I thought you might like it. Would you like to see it?'

'But...'

'It's never been rented out for money and I don't want to do that now, to have someone in it I don't know. My grandparents lived there after we moved and a series of people since and ... it's empty. You're not offended, are you?'

'Offended? Why ... why no.'

The sun was beginning to shine through the window just in time for her day improving.

'Come and look at it,' Sam said.

There was a walled garden right around the building. Once the gate was shut, it was completely cut off from the rest of the town, and it was a real cottage, on the end of the row, and had gardens around it on two sides. It was built of cream stone and had pretty white windows with small neat square panes. Inside, there was a big kitchen, and a sitting room and dining room, and a cloakroom on the ground floor, and the staircase led to two large bedrooms and they each had a tiny bathroom.

The upstairs rooms had views beyond the bottom of the town, and it was all neatly put together, carpeted and curtained, the living room had a wood stove, the garden was filled with sweet-smelling flowers and herbs like lavender and rosemary, and there were trees at the far end and little sheltered places to sit and crazy-paving paths.

The kitchen cupboards were white wood and the cooker was shiny and expensive and the fridge and dishwasher were gleaming white and the wooden floor was spotless. The doors downstairs all had glass to let in as much light as possible and the sun spilled through at the far end of the garden and on to the lawn. There were pots of parsley and chives outside the back door and a silly little stone statue, hiding in among the trees.

Caroline was entranced. She looked doubtfully at him.

'Oh, Sam, I can't take it.'

Sam pressed his lips together rather than say anything.

'I can't,' she said again.

'Look,' he said, 'you've had a very bad time. Why not just accept that something good might happen?'

She shook her head, realizing then how much she wanted to be out of her mother's house, lovely as her mother was.

'Besides, if you're going to work for me, it's so convenient.'

'I work for Stephen in the evenings.'

'You will take it then?'

'Oh, Sam. How on earth could I refuse? I do want a place of my own so much. Are you sure?'

'Quite certain,' he said.

She went over and kissed him. It could have been her imagination or did he hold her just a second after he might have done? No, he wouldn't do that. He turned away in embarrassment, reached into his pocket for the key, told her she could move in whenever she liked. He gave her the key and said, 'Look around on your own. Much more fun,' and then he wandered back into the office and left her there.

She gazed after him for a few moments and then gleefully began a tour of the house by herself.

When she got home and told her mother, she could see how pleased her mother was, but Victoria was even more of a surprise. She blushed and said, 'I'm not coming with you.'

'What on earth do you mean?'

'I'm moving in with Graham.'

This was a shock. She stopped herself from saying anything, but her mother said it for her.

'You've only known him five minutes.'

'As a matter of fact I met him the week I came here, I just didn't tell you, and there's no reason why I should, is there? He has his own flat and I want to be with him. I don't see any reason why I shouldn't.'

She stood there looking defiant and Caroline hadn't the energy to argue and, besides, she was almost eighteen. Why should anybody tell her what to do? So Caroline kissed her and said how pleased she was, and Caroline's mother grumbled slightly and said, whatever would they live on with her working at the teashop and Graham a student, and Victoria said that Graham was finished university and had been offered a job in retail in Newcastle on twenty-one thousand a year and that probably they would move soon. She seemed so grown up and Caroline thought that her daughter had had no option but to become an adult after her father died, and she liked her the more for her good sense but would miss her.

It had not occurred to Sam that he might be prepared to put up a fight for Caroline and, when it did occur to him, he knew that he wouldn't fight as low as to increase her salary or give her the cottage for that reason, but it was a fight of sorts. Even if he never got to touch her again, if he could take her away from Stephen... He was about to think that it would be better if he could take her away, but that would depend on how she viewed being alone. Was having somebody else's husband not better than being alone?

In Sam's experience few men left their wives for other women. Stephen might leave his wife for Caroline. After all, they had no children, but Susan West seemed to him vulnerable. If she had not been, how could she have put up with the move north and his parents and the problems. If she had not loved Stephen very much, she would not have done it. Also, Susan was beautiful and difficult. She was in fact just the sort of woman Stephen would marry and then have problems with.

So, who was at fault? He didn't know. And that was the trouble. When people had decided to divorce, they came to him and said, 'We don't know how we got to this.' Perhaps the problem was almost never of the victim's making, or was not directly so. It was all very well having somebody to blame, Sam thought, but very often it was merely a convenience. People would have loved the neatness of television stories. If they could have put THE END on to their circumstances, what wouldn't they have given to do so, but you couldn't do that. The only ending was death and it was not something many were hurtling willingly towards.

He was disconcerted by Susan and Stephen and even more so by Caroline. He tried not to love her, he did not want to be involved. He wished he could stand outside always and look on. He wanted to sleep at night, because the problems were not directly his and it was part of his job to solve them, but there was something about the way she pushed back her hair, about the way that she turned in the sunlight, smiling when she saw the cottage – he wanted to be objective but he did not know how.

Jess's father had a go at her about Matthew. He caught her outside the flats, perhaps he had realized that she wouldn't let him in, but that didn't stop him from saying the things that he said. Why was it that people you were related to said too much, Jess wondered, why was it that they somehow thought they were privileged, that you would forgive them transgressions you would forgive no one else, that they could trespass upon your soul and you would still smile at them? Why didn't her parents know that she had nothing more to give, that the only words she could have borne were words of support, that she had nothing to hide behind in the event of attack, that her body felt sick and cowardly and that all she could think was how to breathe and how soon she would be inside?

Matthew was away, he had gone to New York so she could not even think that he would be home soon. Meanwhile, her father talked of the shame she had brought on them, of disgrace and betrayal. Her dad was watching too much television, using all those words which meant nothing. She knew that her father loved her. Why did it mean that he inflicted all his ignorance and prejudice and lack of imagination on her?

She stood it. She stood like a sea wall, like the lifeboat withstood the heavy swell, she nodded and said yes a dozen times. She thought that if she did not argue, he would shut up, but he didn't. It seemed that, no matter what she did, it would not make any difference. She was 'having an affair', whatever that meant, with a man who was more successful than anybody else her parents knew, and this was some kind of sin.

After several lifetimes, her father proclaimed that he was washing his hands of her and then he went over to his car, got in and drove away, revving the engine unnecessarily and going at speed. Jess ran for the flat, slammed the door and stood behind it, shaking. Then she slid down on to the floor and the tears began. She wanted Matthew badly but, when the telephone rang and she heard his voice on the answering machine, she hadn't the strength to pick it up or the resolve to call him back. She crept to bed and stayed there with the windows closed, unable even to bear the sound of the tide.

She had been invited to go racing that week. She almost didn't go but, since it was three days later and she had seen and talked to no one, she persuaded herself that she must. Caroline would be there. Sam and Gareth were having a hospitality tent and had invited her. She must try to learn how to go out by herself and this outing should be relatively easy. All she had to do was wear her new Red Cross suit and hat, smile at people, watch the races and concentrate on not drinking too much. That had got easier lately but then she was used to being out with Matthew and when he was there she didn't need alcohol. She finally spoke to him on the telephone and he listened to her woes and then encouraged her to go.

'It'll do you good.'

'But you won't be there.'

'I know. I'm sorry. I'll miss you. Old Sam will be there. You can always schmoozy up to him.'

'Matthew Elliot, I never schmoozy up to anybody.'

'Go. Enjoy it. I'll see you on Friday.'

'You promise?'

'I promise. I love you.'

Twenty-Five

It had been Gareth's idea that they should go to the races and make an event of it. Sam thought it was silly.

'We don't go anywhere as us,' Gareth said. 'We should be seen. We could invite people who would be useful to us. Other firms do it.'

'Other firms are bigger than us.'

'Don't you have clients you care about, that you would like to ask?'

In the end Sam agreed, if only for peace.

Suzan was asked but wouldn't go. Stephen pleaded with her. She looked so wonderful in dressy clothes and, besides, he felt so guilty about Caroline. Susan had done nothing other than not want to be here. And who could blame her for that? He didn't want to be here either, but she said she had once been to a race meeting where a horse had been shot and she was not going to do it again, not even for him.

'I wish you would,' he said.

'Why don't you take Caroline?' she said,

with a thin smile. 'I'm sure she would love to go.'

Caroline was eager.

'I could wear a hat.'

'You have one?'

'I have six. I used to wear things like that all the time.'

On the day of the races, Jess got up early and dressed in her new suit and hat, looked at herself in the mirror and saw a new person, somebody who was not just half of something, a completely separate individual. She had said that she would go alone and meet them in the hospitality tent.

The first people she saw were Alex and Caroline together, so she went over. Caroline was wearing a blue suit and hat and Alex was wearing grey but it was the smell, the perfume, which caught her attention. For a few seconds she did not understand what was happening, it seemed like nothing to do with her or with the day or with the people. It dragged her back to the time when she had thrown out Tom's clothes, the day that she had broken free, that had been such a significant day. It was as though she went back to that day, back before throwing away his clothes, back to the very day when Tom had died. The loss was huge, even worse in a way.

She didn't understand what was happening, she had blocked out something from her mind and it would be kept from her consciousness no longer. She remembered vividly the last few months of her marriage, how impatient Tom had been with her, how often he did not come home, how he was always busy and would be telephoning to say he was going to be late, a day or several days. She remembered how he had not liked anything that she cooked, anything she wore, he was not interested in what she said or did, and the sex – the sex had been awful.

Around her in the hospitality tent people were laughing and talking and drinking champagne. It was a beautiful day, perfect for racing, warm and dry. Outside, the crowds had gathered and the horses were walking round and round the parade ring with owners and trainers, prior to the first race. There were queues for the tote and in front of the bookies' stands and people were up in the grandstand for a better view. Sam was urging her outside, so she went with him. He told her that the best place to watch was along the last straight before the finish. She let him take her arm even though she felt dizzy.

Why had she not let herself remember what those last months were like? Why could she not have admitted to herself that something was very wrong with their marriage? She knew why. It was because it was the only thing she had in her life. No wonder she had been so keen to have a baby, thinking it would hold them together or, if it did not, then at least she would have something real when he walked out. When he walked out? The words echoed and grew huge in her head.

The horses were racing, people were shouting, Sam was telling her that he had bet on a horse called Beyond the Heather and it was sure to win. Around her, people leaned forward in their enthusiasm, shrieking and yelling in excitement. When he walked out? Tom had not been going to walk out, they had had the perfect marriage, it was wonderful. Wonderful.

She thought back but Matthew got in the way. Matthew had seemed wonderful. Was that what she had wanted – somebody to substitute, somebody to fill the gap in her memory, like the missing pieces of a jigsaw that was her life with Tom in Frankfurt. He didn't love her, didn't want her, it had been all on her part, the running, the pleasing, the accommodating. Ninety per cent of everything in their marriage had been on her part.

She panicked. She had blocked all this out and now she had to acknowledge and absorb the fact that her marriage had been failing and was almost over, at least on Tom's side. He had been going to leave her, not like this, not with the silent reluctance of a coffin, but deliberately, at least partly so, perhaps not even consciously at that time but...

The horses' hooves drummed on the grass as they charged past. The crowd screamed, shouted encouragement. Sam was waving his newspaper and even he was smiling.

'We won,' he said.

Alex had been back in the area only a short while when she was asked to spend the day at Hexham races. It was no hardship, she had not sold her house and was now glad of it, and it meant she didn't have to set out very early for work. She didn't particularly want to go racing but, since she was new and they had asked, she felt obliged to smile and say that she would love it.

She didn't know anybody. She had once had friends in the area but they had gone, and the people she had been friendly with when Andrew was alive had let her go because they were couples. She had kept the friends she had who were single or who had known her through business, and she managed a small social life from these. Her work was too demanding for her to make new social contacts other than through work. The trouble was, she thought, spending yet another early evening in the pub in Newcastle, that people who worked together talked about work, so you couldn't get away from it.

She was asked out by various men but didn't go. Some of them were married – she didn't want that again – those who were divorced carried baggage like small children and troublesome expensive ex-wives, and those who hadn't been married were Mummy's boys or losers. She didn't want to get involved with anyone in her business or connected with it.

She hadn't seen Matthew much. She knew that he was away but was surprised he had not rushed back to be with Jess Beardsley. The rumour was that he was everywhere she was, like Mary's little lamb. Alex told herself that thoughts that bitchy meant you were jealous and she should not be jealous of Matthew's relationship with Jess. It was up to him what he did, and if he had found somebody to fall in love with, well, why not? She just hoped it was making them both happy. Jess seemed unhappy, distracted, hanging about Sam Browne as though he might disappear, genie-like, in a puff of smoke.

Caroline McIver was fashionably slender and wore an expensive suit and a gorgeous hat and Stephen West looked as though he was having a fine time without his wife. Gareth's wife was there but Sylvia and Gareth didn't move out of the hospitality tent, even for the races.

Other people whom Alex knew vaguely were there and she managed to impress her colleagues by constantly being greeted and having her cheek kissed, people issuing vague invitations which Alex knew she would never take up.

She wasn't interested in horses or in this kind of competition. She made her way across to where Caroline and Stephen were standing beside Jess. Sam Browne went off somewhere and she said to Jess, 'And how is Matthew?'

Jess looked blankly at her. 'What?'

'I thought I saw you together a week or two ago?'

'Yes?'

Was she ill, Alex wondered. Her eyes were dull, strange and full of confusion, as though she had landed on an alien planet and was lost far from home.

'Did I hear a rumour that Matthew wants to buy the drift mine?' Alex asked Stephen.

'What do you mean?'

'Are you trying to tell me that it's a profitable concern, that it has a future?'

He said nothing and neither did Caroline. Jess was becoming paler by the second. Sweat had broken out on her forehead. Just as Sam returned, she politely crumpled to the ground.

Twenty-Six

It was mid-morning the following day and Caroline was still in bed. Someone was banging the knocker on the front door. She got out of bed, put on a dressing gown and went down to the front door and there stood Jess, her dark hair shiny with rain and her coat collar turned up. Caroline, thinking how Jess had collapsed the day before, tried to persuade her to take off her coat and sit down but Jess wouldn't. She offered tea but Jess refused. She stood in the middle of the floor and looked straight at Caroline.

'I want to ask you something. Were you having an affair with my husband?'

Caroline stared at her.

'Whatever gave you the idea I do things like that?' she said, and then her mind gave her a clear picture of herself with Stephen West on the bed at the pub and her face burned.

'You lived in Frankfurt, we had met, we lived near and our husbands worked together. I could smell your perfume, the one

266

you use. It's the same perfume that I smelled on my husband's clothes several times.'

Caroline shook her head.

'Jess, I don't wear perfume. I'm allergic to it.'

Jess said nothing.

'Whatever gave you such an idea? I loved my husband, I wouldn't have done such a thing, either to you or Tom or to Michael. You couldn't think so. What made you think it? Are you all right? Sit down.'

'No.'

'What makes you think he was cheating on you?'

'I don't know. I think... I should have known you wouldn't do such a thing. I'm sorry. Perhaps I'm losing my mind.'

'I think you're very upset. You had a good marriage, you know that. Tom loved you. This is just because he isn't here, just another form of grief.'

'I think I knew even then,' Jess said. 'I just wouldn't acknowledge it, but if I think about how I have been grieving over him, when he... Can you imagine how you would feel if you thought Michael had? When Tom died, the only positive thing about it was that we had loved one another. If he didn't love me, I have nothing left.'

'I'm sure he did. You always believed it until now. This is just your mind playing tricks because things are so awful.'

'I didn't think things could be this awful. I keep thinking it will get better but it doesn't. I'm not very clever. All I have is my looks and he was the only man who ever meant anything to me. I went to bed with somebody else recently and it was so nice. I feel as if I can't trust anybody now. What kind of woman takes another woman's husband?'

Caroline cried when Jess had gone. She thought about Susan West. In her mind she could see Michael's accusing face. She was supposed to be at the pit office that day, to face the man she had betrayed her husband with. He was not there. She was so relieved. She did the work she had intended to do. It was almost eleven o'clock when she closed down her computer. She was so tired she was dreading the drive back. It was finally dark outside. Just as she was about to put out the lights, a car swept into the yard. It was Stephen's car, she recognized the shape of it in the darkness.

'I was about to leave,' she said as he came into the office.

He looked at her. He looked awful, she thought, tired and grey-faced.

He said nothing.

'You're not going to work now, surely?'

'No. I just ... no.'

'Goodnight then.'

'Goodnight.'

She went out, closed the door, listened to the click-clack of her own shoes as she crossed the yard to the car. She opened the car and put her briefcase and her handbag inside and then for some reason she didn't go. She locked the car again and ran back across the yard and opened the door. Stephen was sitting at his desk with his elbows on it and his hands over his face.

'Stephen?'

He didn't reply.

'Is your father worse?'

'He died this afternoon.'

'Oh, I'm so sorry.'

His father had died and he had watched. His mother and Susan were exhausted because for days and days they had thought his father would die. They had watched for months and they had run out of energy. His father had long since passed into incoherence, probably because of the painkilling drugs which the doctor had administered. How Stephen had needed to get away, to go to work, to have something, some way out. He should not have gone to the races, his mother and Susan had been shocked, but every time he left the house, every time he came back, there was nothing beyond his father's illness, his mother's disapproval and Susan's awareness that they had no money left and that there would soon be the ignominy of having to give up if they were not to go bankrupt and be disgraced, owing people money. The pit would close, the men would be put out of work, the house would have to be sold and they would have nothing.

As the light began to leave the sky, his father took his last long laboured breaths and his body ceased its warmth. By the time the darkness came, his father was dead. Stephen had had to get out for a little while afterwards, he needed the moors, the air was stifling around his home. There was nothing more to be done that would not wait. He had thought Caroline would be long gone. He couldn't bear anybody else or their voices.

'I didn't understand,' she said.

'There's nothing to understand. Should you like me better because my father's dead? I tried to pretend it wasn't happening.

I wanted to be somewhere else, anywhere, anywhere.'

He turned away, choking and breathing over the words he couldn't get out. The choking and breathing was in a fight with what he was saying, and the words were losing. He had thought that if he could keep on talking he would be all right, but the words finally drowned in the wet choking. Even the back of his hands didn't take care of it and it was so disgusting, so humiliating, it was so awful, fighting for control, denying the great wave of black feeling that had taken the whole world.

She drew him out of his seat and over to the old sofa and held him. Her hair stuck to his face. Her neck smelled warm like peaches. She started to kiss him like he wanted her to, like Susan didn't, all over his face, and she kissed his hair. Stephen closed his eyes and let her stroke his hair and hold him. And then she started kissing him on the lips and was concentrating on it. He had thought he would never want anybody to touch him again, but he had been quite definitely wrong about that. The kisses were like notes on a piano, each was different but all in keeping.

It had not occurred to him before now

that Susan never made love to him, that he always had to make the advance, that she expected him to, she liked to receive, she was submissive in a sense, but Caroline had her hands on him in a very definite way.

Susan had loved him once, but selfishly. Some women did that. He remembered a friend once saying that marriage was paying for two dinners in order to get one cooked. Susan had liked his status, his salary. Why had they not parted years ago?

Caroline drew him closer and closer. It was the only place in the whole world that he wanted to be.

Twenty-Seven

Alex lived in a part of the town which was close to the centre but completely cut off in the sense that it was inside gates and surrounded by walls. From the outside, Jess could glimpse the trees, lots of willows and flashy sort of greenery which spread out like a theatre act, sweeping the ground, and there were blinding white criss-cross fences and equally white wrought-iron railings. There were big notices up saying 'Private' and 'Residents Only' and you couldn't get past the gates without stopping and saying into an intercom who you were.

The houses were quite new, with man-icured lawns, and some of them had white pillars in front of them and they were all huge, the kind of thing which would have looked better with an acre or so around it, she thought, and then decided that nothing would make them look better, they were best all bunched together in here like garish blooms in a garden. Jess pressed the appro-priate buzzer and Alex's voice answered and she let her in. The house was enormous inside and had a sort of sweeping hall which went up and up.

'Do you know why I'm here?'

'Is something the matter? Come into the sitting room.'

Jess could smell the perfume. It made her feel dizzy, resentful, as though she wanted to run away.

'I want to ask you something.'

'Ask away. Is it about Matthew? He doesn't like me, if that's the problem. He thinks of me as he might think of a cousin or an aunt. Can you believe that?' Alex laughed. 'He treats me so kindly. Worst of all, I like it. Do have a seat. You're terribly pale. Are you all right?'

'He is very kind,' Jess said, trying to keep in the conversation. Alex was acting very strangely, laughing nervously, uneasy.

'He employs me and sees me occasionally, because I'm his last link with Andrew, so you have nothing to worry about.'

'You had an affair with my husband, didn't you?'

'What?'

'You and Tom, you had an affair.'

The room was suddenly quiet. Jess could see by the change of expression on Alex's face that she was right. The colour drained from her cheeks and her eyes glinted.

'It was going on when he died,' Jess said. 'He went to London quite a lot and that week he seemed to be up and down between London and Newcastle quite unnecessarily. You were there too, it was the week that Matthew's wife died. Andrew and Tom were on the train together because he had been in London for his mother's funeral. You were in London with Tom when Andrew and Matthew were burying Margaret. Weren't you?'

'I can't think how you worked that out,' Alex said.

'I've had a lot of time to think since Tom died, and I see that things had not been right for a long time. Matthew told me that you were away, that you had gone abroad and were out of the country the day of Margaret's funeral but it isn't true, is it? Matthew doesn't know that you were betraying his son with another man that day, and that other man was my husband. It's the truth, isn't it?'

'Jess, you have Matthew.'

'I don't care about him.'

'Aren't you sleeping with him?'

'He's nothing to me. It was Tom I cared about and you took him. You weren't content with having one man, you took mine. He was the only man I ever loved, the only man I ever wanted. You're clever and beautiful and educated, you can have anybody. Why did you take him?'

'I didn't take him,' Alex said, sighing and sitting down. 'It was him. To me he was just fun—'

'Fun?'

Jess understood what was happening. She had died and gone to hell. The rest of the world went on but there was no place in it for her. That was the terrifying part, there was nowhere to be. She was invisible and must be dead, because there was nothing beyond the abyss of her mind. It was being walled up, a permanent sending to Coventry, the stillness of the grave, the silent enclosure of the coffin. Tom was still alive. In some other world beyond, he got on with his life, worked and breathed and had somebody else, somebody like Alex. There was nowhere left for her to be.

'I wouldn't have left Andrew for him,' Alex said. 'I loved Andrew.'

'But he was going to leave me? He was, wasn't he? He would have left me for you.' Jess could feel herself shaking.

'I never agreed to such a thing. I didn't mean any harm. I know it sounds pathetic and I'm so very sorry, Jess. I didn't know ... after all, we're young, I thought we could ... we could play games and it would be all right. I'm sorry. Please believe me.'

Jess left. She drove home, back to the sea, and then she went inside and locked the doors and got out the brandy and turned on the video and when the bottle was empty she opened another and several packets of paracetamol.

Jess threw up. She threw up and threw up until there was nothing to come back up and she was lying on the bathroom floor, hardly able to move, aware of the stench and her misery. The nausea only began to abate when she could vomit no more and all she wanted to do was sleep. Her dreams were full of horror, so that she cried out, at least in her mind, and when she finally awoke, the smell was awful and she couldn't get up. She managed to turn and then, on her hands and knees, she made her way slowly across the floor and into the bedroom. She hauled herself into bed. It was so soft and clean. All she wanted to do was sleep.

When she awoke again she had a raging thirst but felt better. She staggered to the kitchen and drank a glass of water, sipping it in case she wanted to be sick again but it stayed down. She took the glass into the bedroom. There were pills all over the floor, pills which she thought she had taken, and an empty bottle and a glass. She got back into bed, unable to believe that she had tried to kill herself. She was angry, with herself, with Tom, with everybody in the world.

She went back to sleep. When she awoke again it was night time and she was no longer tired and she felt better. She made herself some tea and toast and went back to bed, turning on the television, watching old films. When the morning came, she showered and washed her hair and, since the day was fine, she went for a long walk on the beach. She walked for hours and then she sat on a sand dune at the top of the beach and watched the full tide, and when it began to recede she went across to the shops and bought fish and chips and sat on the front and ate them. They tasted better than anything she had ever tasted before.

It was Friday when Jess came into the office, almost lunchtime. Sam was hoping that it was something to do with her house or her money, something easy and innocuous, but he soon realized that it wasn't. She looked terrible, like a homeless orphan in spite of the expensive cream coat, like an under-nourished, unloved child, her eyes huge and dark enough to cloak the expression in them, and even so she was beautiful, her hair riotous from the wind and the coat enhancing the look of her skin. He offered her a seat but she didn't take it. He knew that was a bad sign. She wandered the office and he waited and then she looked suddenly at him and said, 'Did you know that Tom was having an affair?'

That winded him. Possibilities scurried through his mind like rats.

'Did I know what?'

'Did you know that Tom was having an affair?'

Exact same question, a bad sign. Did he say yes? If he did, she was going to lose her temper, and if he didn't she was still going to, he could see. In the end, past his hesitation, she answered the question.

'You did know. He came to you. I thought he might have.'

'I'm a solicitor,' Sam said. 'I treat everybody the same.'

'Do you take me for an idiot?' she said. Her voice was soft and menacing and Sam tried not to move in his chair.

'You know very well that everything that is said here is said in confidence. You, Tom, everybody.'

Jess slammed down her fist on the desk. She didn't have a big fist but everything on the desk jumped and so did he.

'How could you not tell me? Damn you to hell!' Her fist came down again and her eyes were like needle points.

'What is this, Jess?'

'Don't do that either. You can't get out of it and I'm not leaving until you admit it.'

'I knew nothing.'

'You goddamned bloody liar!'

Sam got up. He was taller than her when he did so, he needed to be. She was looking at him and, if icebergs had had eyes, they would have looked at him like that.

'If he came to you, there was only one reason. He was going to leave me for her. All this time when I was grieving for that bastard, and you let me go on believing that he loved me. You could have told me. Your loyalty to him stopped when he died, surely. Where was your loyalty to me?'

Sam found silence the right refuge.

'What was he going to do, walk out and leave you to pick up the pieces? Was he? You with your wonderful integrity. You devious manipulating bastard!'

'Don't call me names. This is my office.' Sam could feel his own temper beginning to give, and it was a luxury he never allowed himself. He could hear his voice, short and snappy.

'I have confided in you and turned to you and never once did you let slip that you knew Tom was having an affair with Alex Chamberlain–'

'Who told you they were?'

'She did. That he loved her and that he was going to leave me. She didn't love him, of course, no, she loved Andrew, she just liked Tom. She wasn't serious about him, he was just fun. What were you going to do, try to take everything from me because my husband didn't want me any more?' The tears were beginning to well over and run down her cheeks.

'I would never do such a thing and you have no justification for saying it.'

'Even as Tom's solicitor, acting for him, doing your best for him?'

'Tom wouldn't have, and it's not to your credit to say that about him or about me.'

'So, what happened? Didn't you have time to take everything from me before Tom died? How disappointing for both of you. I thought you were my friend.'

'I am your friend.'

'You are neither my friend nor my solicitor from now on. You're low and devious and hateful.' Beside her, on top of the bookcase, were the china birds. She picked up the nearer one and fired it at him. He heard himself shout as she let it go.

'Please, Jess, no!'

The sound of his voice was enough to make her pick up the other and hurl it after the first. They both missed him. One of them hit the middle of the window, encountered the wood and crashed to the floor. The other went into the wall just past his head.

Sam couldn't take his eyes off them. They had been a wedding anniversary gift from his father to his mother and had been in this office for as long as he could remember, in the same place, as though they were about to fly through the window and off into the hills, up on to the high heather. Sam had not cried when Dominic had left him and turned Christmas for ever after into a horror, but he wanted to cry now. He controlled himself, breathing carefully, and then he said, 'Tom came to me and asked if I would act for him, and I said that I would, but I told him to tell you, I told him that you needed a good solicitor, somebody who would be on your side, and he said that he wasn't trying to cheat you, you would get half of everything.'

'You should have told me.'

'When?' Sam glared at her. 'When I was acting as his solicitor? When he died? You think the timing was right somewhere among all this grief? When were you going to be strong enough to hear it? When was I supposed to take away the very support that Tom's love had always given you?'

'You were meant to do it before now.'

'Then I'm extremely sorry that my judgement was so lacking. I do make mistakes sometimes.'

'You could have saved me a lot of heartache.'

'I'm sorry,' Sam said again and after that there was a long silence and in it Sam surveyed the broken pieces of the birds upon the floor. His mother had loved them. 'Get out of my office.' It wasn't so much a request as a threat.

'You shouldn't have done it,' Jess said, in tears.

'Get out.'

She tried for the door and couldn't find the handle. It slipped from her fingers and then she turned it and the door opened.

Caroline had heard the sound of their voices, though not their conversation, from the outer office and it was unusual. Most people had no reason to raise their voices in there and, when the sound of something breaking followed, she got to her feet and was narrowly able to avoid Jess cannoning into her when she left his office at speed.

There was silence. It was not a comfortable silence. There was nobody else around. Gareth was in court, Ivy was making tea in the kitchen and Gareth's new secretary, Tessa, had gone home because her little boy had broken his arm and there was nobody else to take him to hospital. She hesitated for a second or so but when the silence continued she ventured inside. Sam stood as though in disbelief at the pieces of broken china which littered his office.

Caroline waited for him to move and when he didn't she got down beside the mess and examined it closely.

'They won't mend,' she said, trying to say something sensible. 'They're in too many pieces.'

He still didn't move. Caroline went into the kitchen and found a pan and brush and a newspaper and then she went back and shovelled all the bits on to the newspaper. She put them in the bin and then she made Sam some tea and took it into the office. He was sitting behind his desk by then, as though it might shield him from whatever else was going to go wrong. Caroline put down the tray and poured out the tea, gave him a cup and saucer and then she said, 'Why don't you go home early?'

'To what?' Sam said savagely, and then he got up and walked out of the room.

He banged out of the building and didn't come back. Caroline was astonished. Sam never lost control of himself. Half an hour later, to her immense relief, he came back, only ten minutes after his next appointment, but she could feel the suppressed anger coming off him.

Jess drove back to the coast, breaking speed limits all the way. She was grateful to reach the sanctuary of her own place, it seemed that she would not feel better until she could go inside and stay there. She parked the car, got out and heard somebody shout her name and there was Matthew, getting out of the silver Mercedes. How could she not have seen it, glinting in the afternoon light? She considered running inside, except that she needed keys to get in and it would take too long. She waited until he covered the short distance between them. He looked relieved but confused, his eyes unsure but his whole face ready to be overjoyed to see her.

'Jessie!' Lately he had taken to calling her this. She knew it was an endearment, she had heard him say her name like that especially for himself. He had turned her into somebody new. He called her it in the street, he called her it in between kisses, he called her it in between telling her how much he loved her. It was as if he made her more his with every time he used that name.

'I've been telephoning you for days, leaving messages. I was worried. Where have you been?'

There was a part of Jess that saw him coldly, as a successful older man who took what he chose and loved no one, but the better part of Jess saw him as he was. He was hers. This man was her lover, he telephoned, he brought her flowers, he knew the wine that she preferred and bought it for her. He knew how she looked in the mornings. He could bring her body to ecstasy, make her laugh. He had been dearer to her than anyone in her life except Tom. He had been her future.

'I don't want to see you. I don't want to talk to you,' she said.

Matthew Elliot had lived too long to be surprised, she could see by his reaction. He had been let down, disappointed, disenchanted, too many times to believe that his ears might deceive him. A very small smile caught at his lips as though he was amused that he could still be played this way.

'What?' he said.

Jess set off towards the building, moving quickly, trying to get away, hoping that he wouldn't follow her, knowing that she would have to give him some form of explanation.

'What's happened?' He caught up to her as she reached the flats. She didn't even get her keys to the door. She stopped because she had to, and looked properly at him for the first time, and it was so difficult. She had wanted him badly many times, longed for his presence. He had made everything better. He had made everything right, bridged the gap between himself and Tom, healed the wounds, but she was angry because he was there and Tom was not and, although she knew it was misplaced, she could not forgive him for what Tom had done. This man had never been faithful to any woman in his life and she had trusted him, believed him. She could not afford him.

'I don't think you're the right person for me,' she said.

For a few moments he didn't say anything. Jess watched the unhappiness take over his face.

'What made you decide that?' he said.

'I thought about your marriage and the way you treated your family and I decided that I didn't want to take the risk. I don't think you're good enough for me. Did you ever think what it was like for Margaret when you went with other women? Didn't you ever think how lonely she was?'

'Was it something Tom did?'

Jess could have laughed at how clever he was. He wasn't like other people. He didn't see the world in terms of his own perspective. He saw it objectively, not with his own person as the centre of the universe, but as though his mind stood outside everything and coolly calculated. Jess put the key into the lock and ignored him. The moment she tried to step inside, he got hold of her.

'What did he do?'

She didn't answer.

'Jess, whatever he did, it's finished, it's over. It has nothing to do with us now.'

288

Jess looked patiently at him.

'Would you like me to put it differently? Perhaps you could take your hands off me?' She waited until he had. 'You wouldn't believe that I got tired of you, that you're forty – however many you are...'

'Three,' he said.

'That you're middle-aged and we have nothing in common and I got bored?'

'Well, yes, I would believe it if it were true.'

Matthew had discovered something fascinating beyond the glass. Could it have been the rush of waves or the small birds running along the waterline?

'Believe it then,' Jess said.

'I would like to hear the explanation.'

'You don't want to.'

'Yes, I do. Then I'll go away.'

'All right,' Jess said. 'Tom had an affair with Alex. She told me. The afternoon that you buried Margaret, Alex was in London. She'd spent the night with Tom. He was going to leave me. He had a new job in Illinois. I expect he was going to take her with him. That's not what she says, of course. She says she didn't really love him, he was her fun.'

Matthew didn't say anything and Jess knew what she had done. She had not just destroyed her own relationship with him, but she had ruined the only thing he had left of Andrew, his contact with Alex Chamberlain. It had not occurred to her before that, despite the fact that Alex was a complete bitch, Matthew loved her.

Even worse, she had destroyed his own belief that his son had managed the one thing which he had never done – a successful long-term relationship with a woman. Any memories that Matthew had of Alex and Andrew were spoiled for ever in those moments and, if Jess could have taken any satisfaction in hurting Matthew, she would have gained it in abundance. She watched the shutters come down over his face, saw his eyes darken until she couldn't interpret the expression. He looked in fact the way he had looked when she met him. He turned away almost completely.

'I have an appointment in Newcastle. I had better go,' he said.

He didn't shout or accuse or plead. He didn't rev up the car when he got into it or tear along the road to the detriment of the tyres, yet for some reason, as Jess watched the Mercedes out of sight, she expected it to take to the air and soar away into the sky.

Twenty-Eight

It was another month before Stephen, Susan and his mother left Allenheads House. His mother wept and blamed him. Susan blamed him too and she wept. Susan packed everything into tea chests. His mother refused to help. He had found a small house for them to rent in Hexham and transported things there as they were packed. She sat in the dining room and stared out of the windows.

'I'm only glad your father isn't here to see this,' she said.

Stephen couldn't blame his father for what had happened, how cowardly to blame the dead, but he wanted to. Did his mother think a business like theirs could go down in a few short months, or was it just that her pride would not let her admit that for years things had been getting worse?

She had refused to go and look at the new house. He was beginning to think he would have to carry her out of this place, into the car and out at the other end. It was a pleasant little terraced house, small by her

291

standards but well looked after, neatly decorated, and the owner had done everything possible to make sure they would be comfortable. There were shops nearby, the church she attended, she had friends who lived in the next street.

A lot of the furniture wouldn't fit and, since she refused to discuss the subject, Stephen had arranged for it to go to a nearby auction room. She went up to her bedroom and stayed there when the men came for the furniture.

'I don't know how you can do this,' Susan told him.

'What would you like me to do?'

'Other men manage things.'

'Oh, I see, so I'm a failure because my father's business wouldn't work.'

'We are going to live in a horrible little house and what are we going to do, have you at least given any thought to that?'

'I imagined you might stay at the house with her until I can find a job in London and then–'

'And what makes you think anybody will give you a job, you walked out on the last one.'

'I'm not a magician.'

'You certainly aren't,' Susan said and she

walked out of the almost empty sitting room.

Stephen looked around. The men had cleared the sideboard and the big chairs with their leather arms, which had been there for as long as he could remember. All the memories of his childhood were caught up here and there was nothing he could do to keep it. His grandfather had built this house, it had been one of the grandest in the area. His grandmother had built the rockery to one side of the house and his father had laid the crazy-paving paths.

The house was so empty that it echoed. When the auction van had gone and the removal van was ready, he went upstairs to his mother's room and knocked on the door. The sound seemed to bounce off the walls.

'Mother?' He opened the door. The room looked vast without its furniture. To Stephen it was always the room where he had gone as a child when he had nightmares, to be taken into bed with his parents. His father had told him stories in bed and his mother had cuddled him against her. 'We have to go.'

'I'm not going.'

'We have to.' He tried to touch her and she moved away.

'I'm only glad your father isn't here to see what we've been reduced to,' she said. 'He wouldn't have stood for this.'

'Things have changed in the coal industry and that pit was too dear to get any more coal out without buying expensive machinery and–'

'Don't lecture me about mining!' she said. 'What do you know about it? You're a penpusher. You should have been here to help him all along, instead of going off to London like that, and to do what? He loved you. All we had left was this house.'

'He mortgaged it to raise money for the business and we lost–'

'I don't understand all that, I don't want to, all that modern stuff. You young people, you think you invented the world, you think you know everything. So much for education, you can't even keep a roof over our heads.'

'I put all the money I had into keeping it going until he died. That's why we don't have a house,' Stephen said. 'I didn't want him to watch it all go down.'

She was pale.

'Don't shout at me,' she said. 'I'm your mother.'

'We must go. The men are waiting.'

She went off downstairs. Stephen closed

each door behind him before he left. He dropped the keys in at Sam's office. He didn't even look at Caroline. That week he had closed the pit and, now he had the money from the house, he would be able to pay his father's debts, despite the mortgages. At least they were not bankrupt.

Suddenly there was nothing to do. He had not imagined what it would be like, he had not dared, to be as so many men had been over so many years in this area, out of work with no money and nowhere to go. The tiny house was smaller with three of them in it, and the weather was cold and wet. Everything cost money and he woke up in the night, sweating, in the ghastly little back room which overlooked the yard, and wondered what was to become of them. He had applied for jobs in London, written and telephoned people he knew or had known, but nothing had come of it. He understood that. He had got out and it seemed there was no way back in.

Daily, his mind gave him how they had lived in London. Had he loved Susan then? He couldn't think what had happened. She was now as much of a burden as his mother.

After the move, his mother turned into an old woman. Her friends called her but she didn't want to see them and sometimes, if she saw them before they saw her, she would go upstairs into her bedroom and refuse to come out. The stairs in themselves were a problem for her but she managed them quickly if she had to. She wouldn't go out, she didn't even help with the shopping. She sat and dozed over the fire and watched daytime television and picked at her food.

Susan took to cleaning the little house daily. No pit wife had ever had a cleaner cottage than this. He was almost afraid to come home and step on the floor, which was always newly washed. She fussed over wet weather, because she couldn't get the clothes dry, she scrubbed mercilessly at the kitchen cupboards. At night in the back room, mostly she turned away from him. Stephen felt nothing. He had taken his father's ashes and scattered them up on the fells and after that he was numb.

The meals were tasteless, there was not enough money for alcohol and Stephen was aware of the miners on the streets of the village, men he had made redundant. How did they keep their families on the pittance the government provided? On fine days he walked up to the fells and looked across at the pit where his father and grandfather had spent their lives.

There had been so many difficult days lately, the day the men had been paid off and he had left the office for the last time, his father's funeral – some of the men had come to it. Stephen had been ashamed and thanked them and shaken their hands. His mother had ignored them.

He saw Caroline as often as they could both get away. He was so grateful to Sam for letting her have the cottage. He spent most of his evenings there and sometimes half the night. It was the only good thing left in his life.

Twenty-Nine

Matthew and Alex met often at work but avoided one another until a business conference in Newcastle that winter. He tried to pretend that he didn't know what she had done. It had no place here. He had to maintain his composure, be civil, when what he really wanted to do was reach across the table and wring her neck. She was in sparkling form, full of ideas, she looked better than he had seen her look since Andrew's death. He was obliged to put up with her all day, listen to her and try not to pour cold water on everything she said, for the wrong reasons.

During dinner, she ate little, drank less and avoided his eyes. There was a talk after dinner. At the end of it the time was almost eleven o'clock. She left the room hastily.

Matthew was exhausted. People were settling down to make a night of it. He escaped to his own room, listened to the silence, pulled off his jacket and tie and lay down on the bed. There was a soft knocking on the door. When he opened it, she stood there like a condemned prisoner, guilty-eyed and fearful, nothing like the wonderful performance she had given earlier. She stalked past him into the room.

'If you're going to throw me through the window, I wish that you would just do it,' she declared. They were four storeys up.

She was almost crying and somehow it looked ridiculous, because she was wearing a neat black suit, high heels and her hair was cut very short, so thoroughly the business-woman.

'You could have told me,' he said.

'How?' She looked wetly at him. *'I'm terribly sorry, Matthew, but I was screwing Tom Beardsley when I was living with Andrew and now they're both dead and I...* You'd better have this.' She put the key to the cottage down on the table. 'I'll find another job.'

'I never sack people for personal reasons,' Matthew said, walking past the table without touching the key.

'You just sit there and look at them until they can't remember how to breathe. You ruined my concentration.'

'You were doing all right.'

'You're screwing the widow. You always go for the same type, as though you could recreate Margaret, always those empty-headed ones who think you're so wonderful.'

'She dumped me,' he said.

'Do you want me to take the blame for it?'

'Of course I don't.'

'You think it was my fault though. If Tom hadn't had an affair with me, Jess wouldn't feel like she does and you wouldn't have got the backlash of it.'

'He was an arsehole,' Matthew said.

'I always thought he was very like you.'

Matthew looked at her for a second and then he started to laugh.

Alex pressed a fist to her mouth as though to stop any more words getting out and the tears began to fall.

'Oh, look, it doesn't matter,' Matthew said. 'If she'd really cared about me, it wouldn't have made the difference. It was just that I hoped she did. You always think you can start again, recapture the past, and it's ridiculous, and I don't usually feel like that about people.'

'About women?' Alex managed.

'You're right too, I was trying to recreate some Margaret who never existed. How stupid was that?'

Matthew stood by the window and considered the view across the Tyne from Gateshead into Newcastle. He could see the Tyne Bridge, it was a busy view even late at night, car lights and street lights and the river and the darkness of some boat, and warehouses, buildings across the river. You couldn't go back, even to the past that you had invented, and you couldn't go forward to it either.

'How about a drink?' he suggested. 'We could empty the contents of the mini bar.'

She came over and surveyed the fridge as he opened it.

'You don't drink.'

'It's time I cultivated a vice,' Matthew said. 'What do you fancy?'

Thirty

Sam Browne telephoned Stephen.

'Matthew Elliot has asked me to set up a meeting with you. Can you come in?'

That Friday, when Stephen reached Sam's office, Matthew wasn't there.

'He can't come. I'm acting for him,' Sam said. 'He wants me to put a proposition to you. He wants to buy the pit.'

Stephen sat back in his chair across the desk from Sam. He had suspected, even hoped, that this might be the case, and in his mind were all kinds of schemes, the most attractive of which was to run away to London with Caroline and leave Susan and his mother, having no conscience about it, since they would be well provided for, because Matthew was offering some enormous figure. He sighed.

'It isn't for sale. You know that, Sam. It belongs completely to my mother, for all the bloody use it is to anybody. She wouldn't sell it to him even now it's closed down.'

'It would put all those men back into work.'

'She isn't interested in philanthropy,' Stephen said, 'only her own comfort, in fact, not even that on bad days.'

'Matthew says that, if she sells him the pit, he'll give her back the house as part of the deal–'

'Matthew owns our house?'

Sam shrugged.

'God, he is a devious bastard,' Stephen said.

Sam, wisely, Stephen thought, said nothing. How did Matthew know that his mother hated the little terraced house, that he and Susan hated their lives, that such a proposition might attract his mother, giving them back the illusion of what they had before?

'Your mother could have the house and you and Susan could go back to London.'

'I can't leave her there. She couldn't manage. She's turned old and bitter since my father died. She has no spirit. She never goes out, she doesn't want to see anybody.'

'So, you'll talk to her.'

Before he went, Stephen paused in front of the door and turned back to Sam.

'I don't understand why he wants any of it. His brothers worked there but they don't speak to him and he has no happy memories of the village that I'm aware of.'

'Maybe he wants to make a few.'

Jess had tried to go back to watching videos and drinking in the evening but it didn't work. She was bored, she felt sick. She didn't want to spend her time alone at the flat and, although she enjoyed the Red Cross shop, she found herself bored there too if she spent too much time. The women were of another generation, some of them had grandchildren almost as old as she was and, although they were kind to her she had nothing in common with them.

She waited for Matthew to telephone or come back. She started jogging on the beach in the mornings. The exercise and fresh air helped but the days got longer and longer. She went shopping for clothes and make up and didn't buy anything. She had money, so nothing attracted her and she had a lot of clothes anyway and no place to wear them.

She found herself wanting to be at home with her parents but, when she turned up there on a cold winter Friday afternoon, the village was quiet and she remembered that the pit had closed and her father was out of work along with a lot of other people. Her mother, who worked at a supermarket in Hexham, was not at work that afternoon and, when Jess joined her in the kitchen, as the kettle boiled, she asked brusquely, 'So, how is the great Matthew Elliot?'

'I don't know. I'm not seeing him any more.'

'He left you? He would.'

'He didn't,' Jess said. 'I told him to go.'

'Well, that must be a first for him, with all his money. I remember him when he was nowt, getting girls into trouble and thinking he was better than everybody else.'

All Jess could think of was Matthew's eyes darkening when he realized she didn't want him. That was the first time she had thought that his feelings for her were something that might have lasted. She didn't want him even now, she didn't want anybody.

Being at home for any length of time was difficult. Her father barely spoke and the television was on all the time. One of his friends, Philip Elliot, called in. When he saw Jess, his eyes narrowed. He was nothing like Matthew, he was short and fat and wore cheap clothes and looked old.

'So,' he said, 'your boyfriend's trying to buy the pit.'

'Matthew is?'

'Aye.'

'He's not her boyfriend,' Jess's mother

pointed out. 'Gave him the old heave-ho, didn't you, love?'

'A good thing an' all,' Philip said. 'Can you see us working for him?'

Jess's dad had put down the paper.

'Is that right? The pit might open again? I don't care if he's the devil incarnate if I can get my job back. I hate all this sitting about. If he puts money into the place and gets things going again, I'll be well pleased.'

Philip said nothing.

'When did you last speak to Matthew?' Jess said.

'Twenty years ago ... more.'

'How did you find out about him buying the Mary?' Bert asked.

'It's all over the village,' Philip said.

'I wouldn't sell a bag of sugar to that man,' Stephen's mother said when he had explained carefully.

'I see. So, you want to sit here for the rest of your life, do you?'

They were sitting in her bedroom. It was cold up there, no heating, at least they were used to that, she more than anybody. They were sitting on the side of the bed in front of the window. It was the front bedroom, the better one, it looked out over the main street, but in winter it was a dismal prospect, sleet spotting the window, the sky dark and the lazy wind throwing more sleet over the road from time to time. It was her own double bed, which she had insisted on bringing. Stephen didn't blame her for that, but it almost filled the room along with her walnut dressing table and the wardrobe.

In the end, Stephen went downstairs to where Susan was making a pan of broth in the kitchen. She had chopped leeks and carrots, added pearl barley and water, put split peas into muslin and into the pan and cooked a piece of ham. Stephen had two bowlfuls and then he waited for her to say, as his mother and now she always did, 'It'll be better tomorrow of course.'

He had a pease pudding and ham sandwich and left the house.

Susan put a bowl of broth and two slices of bread on a tray and went up to her mother-in-law. She felt nothing but sympathy for the older woman, had become fond of her. Stephen's mother always took her part against him. She waited until the old woman had finished the broth and then she said, 'Stephen tells me you don't want to sell the pit.'

The old lady sniffed.

'I would to anybody of good moral character. It's always been ours, you see, and I don't like to see it not working and the village suffering. If he was a good man, a decent man... He was the death of his wife, you know. Dreadful. And that boy of his. I met him once at the solicitor's. Sweet. Charming. He didn't deserve a boy like that. Sometimes I think God takes people.'

'And he doesn't deserve the pit? Is there anything that would make you change your mind?'

A tear ran down the old lady's cheek. Susan took hold of her hand.

'Shall I tell you a secret?'

'What?'

'I'm having a baby.'

Mrs West's look changed. She began to smile and the smile took over her face and made her eyes shine.

'Oh, Susan,' she said.

'Don't you think it would be nice if I could have the baby at the big house where he belongs and he could be brought up there?'

'A boy?'

'I think we should call him Edward. Would you like that?'

'When?'

'In the summer.'

'I was just thinking this morning, that all the daffodils will be out at the house in the spring.'

Stephen went to Caroline. He didn't tell her what might happen, he didn't want anything to intrude. He had to be careful. It was not that big a town, people might talk and notice. As he walked in the door, she kissed him all over his face. Then she looked at him.

'What's happened?' she said.

He denied it but he thought that was what he loved best about her. She knew something was different. They sat by the fire and he told her.

'Would Matthew want you there?'

'Me? I shouldn't think so.'

'Would you want to be there?'

He did. That was the astonishing part. He didn't really want to leave, he wanted to be at the pit. God, was he turning into his father? He had thought he wanted to go back to London and try to pick up his life, but it was not true. In spite of his mother, he wanted to stay here and to see the pit reopen and to have a hand in it. But the most important reason for staying there was her. He did not think he could live without her.

He could hide in her bed, her arms, her body. She asked for nothing. That peace was becoming an obsession with Stephen, he thought about her all day, he dreamt about her at night and, when he was with her, all he wanted was to have her and talk to her, drink a glass of wine with her. He had drunk expensive wine in exclusive restaurants in the loveliest cities in the world and it did not begin to compare with drinking plonk in bed with Caroline McIver. She made him laugh, she made him want to linger. Beyond her there were devils, blackness, deep pits of freezing slime. Getting out of her bed was always an act of courage. It reminded him of Sunday nights when he was a child, the horrible overhanging feeling of Monday morning to come.

He would go home and Susan wouldn't question him and there was always food and the pretence that stewed steak and rhubarb crumble would keep the world turning. Sometimes Susan even expected sex and sometimes his guilt got him to her. That was when Stephen understood what prostitutes felt like. Born of some apparent necessity, you used something which had not been intended for sale, sinned against creation like this and betrayed the person who you

310

loved, and yourself, but he could not bear Susan's face when he refused. They no longer argued.

The time spent with Caroline was magical. He telephoned her at lunchtime and saw her almost every night. It always felt like the first time, the enthusiasm, the excitement, the eagerness and, like the last time, desperation, regret. He thought that, if they made love every night for the rest of their lives, he would always feel like this about her. He adored her, every breath she took, every word she said. Being parted from her had become hell.

They didn't talk about anything much most of the time, yet they didn't run out of conversation and it was not as though anybody did anything particularly brilliant sexwise, and yet it was all fascinating, brilliant, as high as the stars. It was fearful and wonderful and each time it was amazingly different and reassuringly the same. He hugged to him the idea of Matthew buying the pit and of there being sufficient money so that he might be able to leave Susan and his mother. There had to be a way out.

Sometimes Susan had gone to bed by the time he reached home but that particular evening, even though it was well past eleven, she was waiting for him. She was sitting in their tiny front room doing nothing, just waiting, and when he walked in she said, 'I want to talk to you.'

He had sensed all week that she had something to say. He looked at her. He rarely looked at her any more. He didn't understand why she hadn't left him. She could have gone back to her parents. Instead she put up with him and his mother and the vile little house and his absence. They never talked.

Was she actually going to leave him? The idea rather excited him. If she left him, then he could see Caroline officially. Some of his daydreams might come true, he would have her around him. Things would get better, she could introduce him to Victoria, they could stop hiding and pretending and... Susan was waiting for him to sit down. The chairs in here were so damned uncomfortable, he didn't remember the last time they had sat together. When they were together, it was either while he ate or when they were asleep.

'We're going to have a baby.'

Stephen felt as though somebody had hit him over the head.

'But you can't be,' he said.

'I didn't do this on purpose and God knows, the number of times you ever want me, I shouldn't be, and I know we've been careful, but I am. It's too late to do anything about it or I would have considered an abortion. I'm so out of touch with my body, I had no idea. Our marriage is in a very bad way. You haven't wanted me or anybody since your father died...'

'That isn't true.'

'In fact, you haven't wanted me since before we left London. I don't know what I did or didn't do, but you stopped loving me a long time ago. It was the reason you gave up the work you cared about, the reason you came home. I've done everything I could think of to make you love me but nothing works. You deliberately destroyed everything. You didn't have to put all our capital into a business that was so obviously failing. We didn't have to come here to live. Now we have nothing left.

'I can't have an abortion and I can't go home. I have to stay here with you and your mother and a child I don't want. I hate being poor and I hate you. There is however one redeeming feature to all this. Your mother has agreed to sell the pit to Matthew Elliot if we move together back to Allenheads House and bring up our child there. So, the deal is that, if you want your child, you have to take us back to the house and you have to treat us properly. No running around with other women–'

'I'm not–'

'Oh, Stephen, don't bother to lie. Where did you think I thought you were all these evenings? If you don't behave, I will take your child away and never come back and you'll be left with that dreadful old woman.'

Matthew could remember being small and going past Allenheads House on the bus, although in summer you couldn't see it properly from the road because of the trees around the edge of the property. Sometimes the gates had been open, white gates the same as now. He was not disappointed when he went to see it after he had bought it, it was a good solid stone Victorian house, but it had been neglected for years. It wanted rewiring, the wallpaper was coming off the walls and no doubt bringing plaster with it, the windows leaked and there was an old conservatory which was falling down.

As soon as he could, he found a top company of builders and got them in. He had a new conservatory built, new garages, the garden re-landscaped, the kitchen fitted completely in expensive wood, with a new Aga. By the time he had replaced the windows, the electricity, added central heating, put in two bathrooms, a cloakroom, new doors on all the rooms, replastered and decorated, he was rather pleased with it. He added carpets in a plain almost no-colour, so that they could have rugs added for effect, a security system, electronic gates and garage doors. By the spring, it was finished.

Sam had watched the huge amount of money Matthew threw at the house and had been there several times while the workmen were in, because Matthew was never about and for some reason he wanted Sam to take a look now and then. It had been transformed and yet the essence of the place had not changed. Everything had been done with taste and Sam would have approved if he could have approved of anything Matthew did.

He had been instructed to let Stephen West see it before anything was done with the sale of the pit. That was a good move, Sam thought, and he telephoned and suggested that Stephen might like to take his mother and Susan to see the house and that he would send somebody to let them in, since he had the keys now that the workmen were done.

Sam went through into the main office and said to Caroline, 'Will you show Susan and Stephen West around the house?'

She looked at him.

'Around what house?'

'Theirs. They're moving back in again.'

'They are? Sam...'

'There's nobody else to do it. I'm due in court and–'

'Fine. Give me the keys.'

It didn't occur to Stephen that Sam might mean Caroline, though afterwards he didn't know why he hadn't thought of it and he suspected that somehow Sam knew about himself and Caroline and did it on purpose. At first he had a slight thrill that he was able to come back, and then he reached the top of the drive and Caroline's car was there and any feeling of pleasure left him.

She got out of the car, she was wearing black, which seemed appropriate, but then she often did, and he did also think that perhaps Sam Browne was old-fashioned enough to suggest to his staff that they should wear black because they belonged to the legal profession, or was it just that her

316

instincts were in full working order?

Stephen wanted to leave straight away, to say that he didn't want the house, that the pit was not for sale, or a mistake had been made. Caroline's scruffy little white car was badly rusting round the windows and the edges of the doors and looked grubby. She greeted them politely, fitted the key into the front door, and they stepped inside. It smelled new and he could almost imagine what it would have been like if he and Caroline could have gone to view a house as a couple, a house which had just been built.

There was stained glass in the hall window, Matthew had had sufficient taste not to touch that, Stephen thought, and somehow it shone, even on this dull day. The wooden floor was oak and had been stripped and polished, and the staircase had also had attention, it went up in three parts and dominated the house. The central heating was on and there was a blast of warm air to meet them. His mother chuntered about how different it was but he could tell that Susan was pleased. She cooed over the Aga, loved the bathrooms, hurried from room to room like a child with new toys.

There were double doors between the dining room and the sitting room and they were both lovely rooms, big and wide. Stephen couldn't fault what had been done, he could only imagine the huge amount of money it must have cost and wonder why Matthew had spent so much when it wasn't necessary. Was that good business or was it just that Matthew's creative instinct had bettered his business sense? Stephen looked out of the window at the lawns and gardens, the trees at the far end, beyond which was a field and beyond that was the fell and beyond that was the sky. He left them and went outside and Caroline followed.

Does every woman dream of owning a house like that, detached so that you have grounds with gates and a drive, with privacy and comfort, prosperity, views, big square rooms, a man, and children and a future? It seemed to Caroline like a fairy tale, it was built so boldly, so high, big stone blocks and lots of space around it, giving it presence.

She had never owned a house, always rented them, and not a big place like this. She knew that most women had never had a house like this, but it didn't make her feel any better. It was too late for her, her husband was dead, her child was grown, but she could not stop thinking about it, friends invited to dinner on Saturday nights, a huge log fire in the sitting room, laughter and talk and red wine as thick as berries.

The kitchen at Allenheads House had two windows and old-fashioned cupboards built into the walls, and you could see from there the back patio and fruit trees in the kitchen garden and the big porch at the back of the house and the garages beyond. From the hall at the other side was another room which would have been a study and then up the stairs with a window halfway, on up to the bedrooms, children half asleep in warm beds and adults with secrets.

She followed him outside. The rain had increased. When she had driven through the middle of town, the scenes beyond the car were all smudged like a Monet painting, coloured squares sliding. She had had to drive slowly and the windscreen wipers made their sing-song way across the glass and people seemed to drip into one another and the grey buildings ran free and cars slicked their way through the streets.

In the garden of the house which the West family had built and owned, the rain was a downpour, so there was no chance that the old lady or Stephen's wife would venture out. Caroline had left her coat in the car and was drenched within seconds. The water ran down her hair and her face and through her clothes.

She could see Susan West watching her from the house and could tell by the expression on her face that she knew Caroline and Stephen were having an affair. It's no good, Caroline thought, I can't do this to her.

Stephen stood while the rain plastered his jacket to his shirt and his shirt to his body and his fair hair to his head, so smoothly that the water ran down his face and ears and on to his neck and the collar of his shirt. He almost said a dozen things and discarded them as unworthy of speech before they reached his lips. All he wanted was to be in bed with her as they had been so many times. He wanted to run away from the problems, he was tired of facing up to everything.

He knew now what it was about her that he loved best. It was the way that she didn't lean on him. His mother and Susan sucked at his energy, snatched at his shadow. Caroline renewed him, made him feel better. He considered what it would be like to live here with her, to have a house such as this, to sit in the garden with her in summer, to have a meal with her each evening, to sleep in her

320

arms with the windows open, to be able to contemplate the future with some kind of equanimity.

'Caro–'

He met her eyes.

'Susan is pregnant.'

After that he couldn't even say her name.

'You do want a child,' Caroline said. 'Your mother must be pleased, and she'll sell the pit to Matthew and you'll have the house. People are entitled to another chance. You're lucky. Take it.'

He got hold of her and pulled her under the nearest tree, where he had played as a child.

'Let's run away,' he said.

Caroline put a hand into his wet hair.

'There's nowhere to run to,' she said. 'And, oh, Stephen, having a child is the best thing in the world, the hardest, the most heartbreaking and the best. Don't spoil it.'

He kissed her all over her face and then she made him let go.

She moved away from him down the garden path. He watched her red hair and her firm steps as she walked towards the garden wall at the far end. The rain had outlined her body where his hands had been so much at home. It was the first time that he had felt lost in this place where he had been born.

He walked slowly back up through the rain to the house and when he got there his wife was standing by the window. She turned around.

'Is it over?' she said and for the first time in many months he felt sorry for her. Her eyes were full of fear.

'How long have you known?'

'Almost for ever,' Susan said and her voice wobbled. 'Do you love her?'

How could you tell your wife, when she was pregnant with your child, that you loved another woman? He couldn't. He was not quite the bastard who would do that. While he was still trying to reply, Susan said, 'Would you have left me? I didn't want this baby, Stephen, I–'

He took her into his arms and told her lies, because there was nothing else to be done and because this had been his fault, somehow all of it. They would have this baby and it would grow up in the house where he had grown up and, if Matthew would let him, he would run the mine. That was what was supposed to happen, he thought, it had just taken him such a long time to work it out.

Thirty-One

Stephen was surprised to find Matthew instead of Sam when he went to the solicitor's office. Matthew was sitting behind Sam's desk as though he belonged.

'So,' Matthew said, 'what did you think of the house?'

'My mother says she will sell you the pit, though you're robbing her.' He stopped there because Matthew laughed.

'She would say that,' he said. 'Will you run it?'

It was the only thing Stephen had wanted him to say. To have it said so easily made him think that Matthew had somehow known what he wanted to hear.

'Are you going to pay me reasonably?'

'Stephen...' Matthew got up and came to him as though they were friends, it was quite alarming that Matthew was genial. He must be so very pleased about it. How strange. 'I will pay you handsomely.'

'There's no need to go too far,' Stephen said, 'let's sort out how much you'll pay for the pit first and then we'll discuss the rest.'

For several weeks after the sale was negotiated, Matthew stayed away, but, once Stephen and his family were settled back at Allenheads House and Stephen had opened the pit again and taken the men on, Matthew was aware that he should go north and talk to Stephen about the many changes he planned to make. Only cowardice kept him away. He tried not to work out how many years it had been since he had left, but, the minute that he drove his car up the steep narrow winding road towards the village, the years all dropped from him and he could see himself and Margaret leaving – she was in tears and Andrew was asleep on the back seat of the car.

He tried to avoid looking towards the little house where he had grown up or any of the houses where his brothers lived with their families. He did not think about the streets where he had played when he was a child, but a thousand memories crowded in on him by the time he reached the gates of the pit. He left the car and walked into the office.

He wanted to decline Stephen's offer of a look round but he knew that he ought to see everything, if only for his face's sake. He prayed that none of his brothers would be there, but one of the first men he saw was his brother Philip, and after that he could concentrate on nothing. He just wanted to leave, couldn't think why he had ever taken this on. He spoke to Philip and Philip nodded back at him, though he didn't say anything. Their eyes met and it was enough for Matthew to understand to its fullest extent what he had missed all those years.

He and Philip were the two eldest children, there was only eighteen months between them. They had slept in the same bed, plodged in the stream, caught tadpoles in the pond, gone to school together – they were even in the same class once every two years when Matthew caught up. They climbed trees for birds' nests, had conker fights, fought one another's battles at school, he in particular, because Philip was not good with his fists and not as tall as Matthew. They had lain together, listening to their parents having drunken fights, and now there was not even a word between them. Matthew said yes and no at Stephen while his insides suffocated and died. He had loved Philip so very much.

All he wanted was to get away but he

couldn't, he had to give a decent amount of time, both in the pit and the office. By the time he had been there two hours, he had a massive headache, a terrible weariness and an overwhelming desire to get into his car and put as much ground between himself and this place as possible. He had to stay. He endured their idea of lunch, a sandwich in the office and some appalling coffee, but in front of him all the time was his brother's image. Philip was so down at heel, so fat, his face creased and lined, his eyes all-seeing. He had a wife and three children. Matthew had not met any of them.

He finally managed to get away and there, just to complete things, was Jess, just beyond the gates.

Jess had put her flat on the market. It seemed pointless to keep it, she was there so little that it was not home any more. Home was her parents' house, the flat looked so lonely when she went there, and she felt the depression hit her when she walked in. There was no sound, no atmosphere, nothing to welcome her. She would collect what she had come for and scurry back to Burnside as though she was being chased.

Her parents' house had become a sanctuary. There was rarely silence. Her father was back at work and her mother worked different shifts, part time, so she was very often at home, and Jess liked the company. Also, her mother spoiled her, she had nothing to do, it was like being a child again. Her mother did all her washing and ironing, made the meals she cared for most. Jess would lie in bed each morning and her parents did not ask her to get up or do anything, as though sloth was part of the healing process, or as though they had at last realized what she needed.

When the weather was fine, she went for long walks up the road on the moors. Sometimes she even went out and walked miles in the bitterly cold wind and rain, but as long as she had waterproof boots, leggings and coat, it didn't matter, and she knew the area too thoroughly to go off the well-known tracks and get lost.

She didn't always want to go. Her father, in some wisdom, had bought a dog, a labrador crossed with something else, and it was an animal which would walk all day. The company of the dog was enough, it didn't bore or distract her with talk and neither did it run away, but seemed happy dashing about no matter how far she walked, and then would lie at her feet by the fire in the evenings after a big meal.

At night she would fall asleep happy in the knowledge that her parents were near and nothing could harm her. She slept long and well in the room next to them and was glad to hear them moving about and the low sound of their voices when they went to bed. The sounds and sights of her days were all those of her childhood, her mother still washed on a Monday and did the ironing in the afternoons. She baked on a Saturday, made a roast dinner on a Sunday, turned out the house on a Friday in time for the weekend, and Jess revelled in the reassuring regularity of it.

She wanted nothing else. She was content to go to the pub with her dad for the odd pint, to wave and speak to old friends on the street.

She was glad when the dreadful day came which was the anniversary of the accident, and she was at home with her mother and father and they didn't leave her all day. They didn't say much other than to tell her that they had not forgotten, that they never would forget, and they kept her close and Jess felt the support and was comforted. She went for a walk with her dad in the afternoon and, when they watched the sun setting, she felt as though she had put something behind her.

'A year and a day clears all debts,' her father said.

She knew what he meant. Perhaps now she would be able to go forward, to remember when she had been happy with Tom, but to think of herself, because it had been long enough to grieve over a marriage which had been far from the perfection she had once imagined. It had been good once, nothing lasted for ever, Tom was dead and she was not. She had people who loved her, she had a place here on earth, a home, comfort and a future.

When she went to the pub, young men looked admiringly at her, but after one or two had approached her and been rebuffed, they learned to leave her alone. She didn't want to go to the cinema or to a dance or anywhere noisy or closed in or where she would meet lots of carefree careless people her own age. She felt older than them, the gap could not be filled, with their inexperience of life, so she stayed at home when she had walked half the day.

At first she was glad to be rid of Matthew and then she listened to the people in the village talking about him, what a devious horrible person he had always been, even when he was young. His brothers called him vile names and spat in the street when they spoke of him. When the pit was sold, Jess dreaded the sight of Matthew's silver car or the way that she might meet him, but he didn't come to the village.

Stephen West was always at the pit, his green Range Rover was to be seen at all hours of the day and night and at weekends. Jess was haunted at first that she might see Matthew, and avoided the area as best she could, considering that she lived there. He did not change the name of the pit but his wagons had Elliot written on them, black on white, what else, Jess thought, and they went back and forward from the pit with coal. The men had their jobs back and her dad stopped sitting about, muttering, and went off to work with a smile on his face.

'I thought he'd never liked it,' Jess said.

'Aye, well, it's what you call a love/hate thing,' her mother said. 'Besides, it's a man's pride still to put food on the table, and it does mean I don't have to spend any more time than necessary in that bloody shop.'

Jess tried to talk her mother into letting her pay for things, but her mother wouldn't have it. Jess told her that she had a lot of money, but her mother said she would have need of it later and would not accept more than a few pounds board from her daughter each week. If she had been a millionaire, they would have taken nothing, because they were her parents.

Jess soon convinced herself that the village was right about Matthew, he was not the kind of person she wished to associate with, and she built up this picture of him in her mind as somebody like her father's friends, middle-aged, opinionated, all right to talk to but never in the world fanciable. In the pub, she watched them and cast him in the same role. He was no different, he just had more money. She couldn't think what she had ever seen in him and, whatever it was, she saw it no longer.

Men that age were a different generation, they were nothing to do with her, they cared for football and darts. She was disgusted with the idea that she had gone to bed with Matthew, and tried to convince herself that she had not. She tried to think of any of the other four Elliot brothers that way and couldn't. They had thick accents, bad teeth, terrible hair if any, and shabby clothes. Matthew was an insult to his generation, picking up young girls, thinking that he might still attract them, acting like somebody twenty-five. She was glad to be rid of him.

She was walking past the pit gates when she saw him, pulled up sharp as she looked along towards the offices. The silver car was parked nearest to her, impossible to miss, dirty as though it had come a good many miles, covered in muck and salt, the number plate almost indistinguishable, and to her dismay Matthew walked out of the building, a briefcase clasped in his hand. It was too late for her to avoid him, she could not run and he had seen her. He walked slowly across the distance between them and Jess was amazed. He was wearing a dark suit and a white shirt. He looked so rich and she had forgotten that he was very good-looking. He also seemed completely out of place. Jess was immediately aware that she was a mess, a woolly hat pulled low over her brow against the wind, her mother's grey and red anorak, a pair of disreputable jeans, and the dog prancing at her feet.

'Hello, Jess, is he yours?'

He got down to the dog just as though his suit had not cost several thousand pounds, and, hearing his soft voice, the dog went to him and Matthew talked to it, tickled its ears, told it how wonderful it was and smiled. 'Nice to see you,' he said, and then he turned around and walked to his car, threw the briefcase in at the back, pulled off his jacket and got in and drove away.

It wasn't until then that Jess realized she hadn't spoken a word. She was shaking, almost crying, her defences were gone. She had given up this man and he looked as though he didn't care. He had been polite and that was all. She turned away, her throat aching because she couldn't cry, but the images of him wouldn't go away. There was a huge widening gap which he had left. She was filling that gap with her parents and friends, her home and this dog.

She ran. She pulled around her the effects of her home life like a duvet when she had flu. She tried to recreate the comfort she had known before she saw him but it was gone. Nothing helped, nothing eased the pain of his departure, watching the silver car out of sight, seeing his face again and again, his friendliness, his ease. Jess panicked. She saw how small her life was, she saw that she had given him up because she was afraid. And she saw that Tom had been the cause of it, but she understood now that she could not have Matthew and her family and she had already made her choice.

Thirty-Two

It was the hundredth anniversary of the Sunny Mary. Stephen's mother was forever reminding him and Susan and anybody else who would listen. She didn't seem to think that it was indelicate, since the pit was no longer theirs, nor care.

Stephen and Matthew were in the office. The rain was pouring down the windows. Matthew was for once in a fairly good mood.

'Do you think the men care about the anniversary?' he said.

'Of course not,' Stephen said crisply. 'It's just that coal has been mined in this area for that long, it's not essentially about us. All they care about is their work and being paid.'

'Yes, but ... we could have a party at the High Moors Hotel.'

The hotel he mentioned was the best in the area, between Hexham and Newcastle. It had been the home of an old Northumbrian family and was set in big grounds.

'Just so long as the pit doesn't have to pay the bill,' Stephen said.

'I'll pay the bill. They can all bring their wives and we'll invite anybody who has anything to do with the business.'

Jess had had to be persuaded to go to the party, but she did not want to seem too reluctant, that would have set her mother thinking that she still cared about Matthew Elliot, and Jess had to make sure that people knew she didn't care whether he was there or not. Matthew would be obliged to put in an appearance, people felt sure that was all he would do, he was nothing to do with the history of the place, he was the new owner, his very newness was against him in this respect, though Stephen West assured everybody that Matthew's money would pay for everything.

Jess's father and mother and all their friends would be there, so she had to go. So would the four Elliot brothers and their wives and everybody from the village who had known Matthew when he was young. It was a lot for him to face, she thought, but she knew that he would. He was not the person to back down from difficult encounters.

In defiance, Jess wore the plain black dress

she had worn the night they met, without make-up or jewellery, and her hair quite plain, short and pushed behind her ears. Her mother looked hard at her.

'A funeral, is it?' she said.

It was a fine summer evening. Buses had been hired so that nobody would have to drive. The hotel itself was a place she and Matthew had gone to several times, once for afternoon tea and a couple of times for dinner. A huge room had been set aside and here Stephen West and his wife and mother were making people welcome. There was champagne if you wanted it, though most of the men declined.

Matthew was not there, or if he was Jess couldn't see him. She spotted Gareth and Sylvia, laughing and talking. They didn't see her and it was easy enough to ignore them. A band was playing softly. The hotel had wonderful views clear across the valley which it looked down on, and the village below. All Jess could see was the difference between the land and the sky, darkness, the lights twinkling in a friendly fashion below.

As she gazed from the window, Caroline and Sam came to her to say hello and Caroline hugged her, told her how well she looked, and Jess knew that it was so. She had not needed make-up or jewellery. She had looked into her mirror and seen a heart-whole person, a recovered image, somebody young and fresh, who ate properly and got lots of exercise in the pure air of the fells. Her skin glowed, her eyes sparkled, her hair shone, she didn't need artifice, the black dress was dramatic and, if it could have improved on her looks in its expensive simplicity, it did. She thought that Caroline looked tired and Sam looked well, just like himself, he didn't alter.

And she saw Matthew, wearing a dark suit that made everybody else look shabby. He didn't see her or, if he did, chose not to acknowledge her. He was talking and smiling and Jess actually saw Mrs West take Matthew's proffered hand and it made her want to smile too.

'Mrs West. How nice to see you,' Matthew said.

'It's so kind of you to provide a party for my husband's men,' Mrs West said.

'Not at all. It was my pleasure. Do you know Alex Chamberlain?'

They shook hands.

'Perhaps you would like to dance?'

While the old lady tried to think of some

way to refuse, Matthew put a hand under her arm and guided her off towards the dance floor. Alex tried not to smile.

'That was very bad of him,' Stephen said in her ear.

'I'm sure he's met his match in her.'

'They're both bloody awkward. Can I get you a drink?'

Susan West was wearing a dress that Alex would have died rather than wear, it managed to make her look dumpy, being white at the top and black all the rest of the way down. She looked haggard, as though she lacked sleep, as though she would have given a great deal not to be there, especially since her rival was just across the room.

Alex watched as Matthew guided Mrs West expertly about the floor. She wondered how many years it was since Stephen's mother had had an attractive man's arms around her. The poor woman began to respond to what he was saying. At the end of the dance he did not relinquish her to her son and daughter-in-law as Alex felt sure he must be keen to, he took her away to the bar, chatting amiably as far as Alex could see, until Mrs West actually laughed and then they danced again and the old woman seemed completely lost to whatever charm he had chosen to employ. Alex felt very sorry for her. She must have been a beauty in her day.

It was unfortunate that, for the women of her generation, all they had was their looks, and when that was lost they had nothing, because there had been little education, no entry into interesting work, no advantages, women sold themselves like paintings to the highest bidder.

Mrs West had done all right in a backwater. In London, no doubt she would have caught the attention of someone richer, more influential, but then men didn't always marry women they desired. Unless Mrs West had had background, she might not have made it to the altar at all, so she had been lucky. Alex shivered and thanked God she hadn't been born any sooner.

When the dance ended, Sam went off to rescue Matthew from Mrs West. He led her away towards the food, and Caroline could see them there while he tried to tempt her to various delicacies. She shook her head at first but Caroline could have told her that it was no good. Sam was used to dealing with people, old ladies were no problem, particularly at a party like this. Caroline wanted to go home. She had wanted to go home from the moment she got there and saw Stephen and his wife and his mother.

The noise was tremendous as people enjoyed themselves, all she wanted was to go home and get into bed and pretend that she had never seen Stephen West. He danced with as many different women as he could in his capacity as pit manager. She wondered whether he was enjoying the work. He looked happy. She could not help hating that. Sam danced with lots of different women and so did Matthew. Jess disappeared. Caroline searched the ladies' room, the foyer, and finally the garden, and found her outside, with a glass of champagne in her hand. Caroline tried to get her to come inside.

'I didn't think Alex Chamberlain would be here,' Jess said miserably. 'She's with Matthew.'

'I don't think she's really with him, she's just–'

'What do you mean, "really", either you are or you aren't, and she is, I can see by the smug look on her face. What is he doing with her? She was his son's ... lover. It's disgusting, that's what it is.'

'They're both free,' Caroline pointed out.

'Free?' Jess looked into Caroline's face. 'She takes everybody. First Tom and now–'

'Jess, you gave him up,' Caroline said firmly. 'You told me that, didn't you?'

'It was because of Tom, it wasn't anything he did. I just couldn't stand anybody–'

'I know.'

'Why does she get everything she wants?'

Caroline understood. She could see what she wanted across the floor but she hadn't even the right to speak to him. How had she let Sam talk her into coming, when she knew that Stephen would be there with his wife and mother? She had thought – at the back of her mind she had thought that she would feel better, that she would see him as a husband and son and remember that he would become a father soon, and it would be all right. It would be cathartic, only it wasn't. It was awful.

Matthew considered he was doing well to stay upright. He couldn't remember what he had said the moment after he had said it and was surprised when people did not frown or show confusion. He had no idea what any of the conversation was about. All he knew was that his four brothers were there with their wives and some of them had their children with them. He did not know any of these. He couldn't go to them, he couldn't even wish

341

them good evening. He danced. He might even have danced with one of their wives. Some women made conversation, some didn't, and he had no idea who they were. Perhaps they didn't know what to say. He became very tired, trying to talk all the time and smile and dance and say all the right things to all the right people.

There were a lot of people at the party, so most of the time he couldn't see any of his brothers. They avoided him, of course, and probably they wouldn't have let their wives dance with him. If he had been unfortunate enough to ask any of them, they would have refused, just like girls refused in the old days, with a shake of the head and without meeting your eyes, so it was safe to think that he had not.

Whenever he glanced around to see if Alex was alone, she was chatting or dancing or laughing, eating, drinking, just as though she was having a good time, when in fact she had not wanted to be there. People would talk, she said. He listened to her objections, that it was work, that it was nothing to do with her, that she was busy, that she had a conference to go to.

'Please,' he had said.

'Why do you need me?'

'Because my family will be there and they don't speak to me.'

'Then why do it?'

'The Wests want it.'

'They don't even own the pit any more. What on earth do they have to do with it?'

'It's owing,' he said. 'Come with me, please.'

So she had and he was grateful and as long as she wasn't left alone they would get through the evening.

Jess and Caroline came back inside and the first person they saw was Stephen and he asked Caroline to dance. She had anticipated this and had tried to imagine that she would turn him down. All she had to say was 'no'. The trouble was that she didn't remember how. Her mouth would not frame the word, her tongue went solid. She had missed him, she wanted to tell him how much, that the lights had gone out, that the world was a nasty, lonely, unforgiving place without him.

In a way it was enough to see him, to see him wanting to dance with her, to be close in the only way they could respectably be so, to be aware that he had looked for her, waited for her, even been ready to be jealous, men were so good at that. Worst of all, the band were playing 'Danny Boy', so slowly, and people were close in each other's arms. It might be your last chance ever, her mind told her. Nobody had asked her to dance all evening. In her hardest moments, she believed that no one would ever ask her again, that she and not old Mrs West would go to the grave unwaltzed and unheld.

All she did was nod and after that she was in his arms and it was so much better than even the best that she had kept in her mind. How could she ever let him go? He drew near and she closed her eyes and only when the last strains had died away did she move back.

He had to leave her. She could see Susan West at the edge of the dance floor, watching and waiting for him. Blindly she found the open doors, stayed outside until she was certain she was not going to cry, and then she went to the ladies' room and stayed there for a long time, listening to people's chatter and sitting on a stool in front of the mirror, doing her hair and wondering if it was late enough to go home.

It was the last dance of the evening. Jess had not realized until it was announced and when it was she watched Matthew Elliot come all the way across the floor to her and, in front of his family and her family and all the people he employed and all the people who didn't like him, he said to her, 'Will you dance with me?'

So she did. Several times lately her mother had said, 'I wish you would find a nice lad your own age,' implying that it was Tom's age to blame for his unfaithfulness, and that anybody above thirty was therefore bound to do the same. Most mothers would have been pleased that their daughters seemed able to attract successful men, but she knew – and it was amusing in one way – that all her mother wanted was for her to marry a local lad, preferably somebody from the village, settle down in a terraced house, for him to work at a factory or some such, for them to have a couple of children and for everybody to live happily ever after. It was what all her mother's friends' children had done, and she had seen her mother looking wistfully at their grandchildren.

Her mother wanted her to live near, so that they could see one another every day, and for her dad and her husband to have things in common, so that they could discuss football and go to the pub and have that close family existence which so many people around them had. Her parents had had nothing in common with Tom, she knew they had felt awkward around him, her mother in particular felt that Tom had stolen her away and, although her mother would not have admitted it, they liked having her back, they liked being able to comfort her, they had perhaps been glad in an obscure way that Tom had betrayed her, because it proved that he was not one of them, that he was not an honest working man, whatever that was. She was quite sure lots of supposedly honest working men betrayed their wives and worse.

Her parents did not believe in education, they believed in hard work, earning a wage, coming home to your loved ones at the end of the day. Her mother would not have gone out to work if they could have afforded her to stay at home, they did not believe that women should have to work, it was shameful that they should do so, it should be enough that they had children and a home, a clean house and cooked meals. They did not understand needing friends other than family, that Jess had been happy living in another country with her husband.

The man who was waltzing her so expertly

about the floor had never fitted here nor would he ever. They did not understand him and possibly he did not understand them. She could see her mother watching anxiously. Every pair of eyes in the room was watching. Other people stopped dancing and moved back. Matthew either didn't notice or didn't care. He held her lightly as though they were mere acquaintances and did not talk to her.

He had saved the pit, the livelihoods of each one of them, and they disliked him for being that clever. She did not understand why he had done it and did not dare to ask. As the music faded, he stopped and thanked her and moved away, smiling just a little.

She walked back across the room, watched by her family and the Elliot family and all their friends. As she got back to them, her mother hugged her.

'Let's go home,' her mother said. 'The buses will be here soon.'

Jess put on her coat and went with her family as the big blue and white buses pulled into the car park.

Caroline had gone outside, wanting to cry, but when she got there Sam came out to her.

'Are you all right?'

347

'No,' was all she said.

'I'm so sorry that it didn't work out.'

She turned in surprise at the sensitivity.

'How did you know?'

Sam looked down.

'I've always known,' he said. 'And I made you go and show them around the house and–'

'She's pregnant. I couldn't take him from her like that. Oh, that sounds awful. I think it will work out. They have the house and the baby and the pit and... Some people get so much. We did. We had everything. We were so lucky,' she said.

'Do you want me to take you home?'

'I'm fine,' she said, embarrassed, and moved away.

As Alex and Matthew got into the car when the evening was over, he said, 'Would you mind if we drove to the cottage?'

She didn't want to go, it was late and she had nothing with her other than a lipstick, her keys and a credit card, but she didn't want to argue. Her house was just up the road, the cottage was almost an hour away.

He drove very fast, nobody spoke all the way there and, when they arrived, he unlocked the door but did not go inside. Alex followed him on to the beach.

That week at the pit, Matthew had come face to face with his brother, Philip. Philip had actually smiled at him.

'Now, Matt,' he said.

That was all, two words and a smile. Matthew's heart had fairly resembled a seagull launching itself off a cliff top over a wide bay, but he knew better than to smile back. He said, 'Now, Phil,' just as though it happened every day, and he got back into his car as he had intended and drove away.

Alex took off her three-inch heels. They were very expensive and she had no intention of ruining them in the sand. She left them at the top of the beach, the sand felt cold on her bare feet. The tide was well down. He was standing at the water's edge. There was a huge moon, casting its shadow on the almost still sea and glinting on the rocks.

'You can't ever have belonged there,' she said.

Matthew looked sideways at her and then he sighed.

'No,' he said. 'I didn't. The Elliots took me in for money.'

Alex came close and put an arm around

him, she tried to do it casually but she knew
he needed the support.

'Why?' she said.

'My father had died and my mother was
getting married again. He mustn't have
wanted another man's child.'

Alex knew better than to attempt comforting words. She put her other arm around
him. She kissed him on the cheek a couple of
times until he turned and kissed her full on
the mouth. When she didn't respond he
stopped and looked at her and said, 'That's
not OK?'

'Actually, it is.'

'We don't have to–'

'Let's,' she said.

'Alex–'

'Look, I like you a lot and I want to go to
bed with you. It shouldn't be such a novelty.
Lots of women have, yes?'

'Only because I make money.'

She laughed.

'There's nothing wrong with money,' she
said.

Jess had smelled of cold heather and the
stream beyond the village. It made him
think of being a child and other people's tea
times, warm cake and melting butter and

350

hot tea. She would have that at her mother's house, she carried the past on her like a prayer and it was something he had never stopped longing for, the gathering darkness, the lights from the house and the mother calling the children in from play.

He had wanted it so much, to hear his name called into the fast fading grey, to run into the kitchen where the cloth was laid upon the square table in front of the window, for the fire to be high and orange and the table to be laden, the plates and cups and saucers all winking in the firelight, the cutlery neat, and in the middle of the table, jam glistening like jewels in little glass saucers, and bread and butter piled up all golden and white, and custard tarts and egg-and-ham pies, the kind where the eggs were put in whole and the ham in square chunks. And little cakes with white icing tops, and pink blancmange and red jelly and a great big brown teapot, all fat and dark, ready to spill steaming tea into the blue and white china cups where the Japanese bridge separated the lovers, and birds were united high above.

It was never like that in the Elliot house. Theirs had empty beer bottles under the table and a used smell, ashes and grit and oilcloth sticky from feet, the backyard was full of bits of things and the table was bare. And he had realized that he could not have any of that now, it was too late. Jess had been nothing but an illusion, the person he had hoped Margaret might be, but he could not be anything other than an outsider in the village and Jess could never accept that.

It was different with Alex. She was his equal in every way and somehow he had always known it.

Epilogue

It was a fine September day in Hexham. From his window, Sam Browne could see the sun shining across the hills. Stephen West's mother had died and Stephen was due in the office that day.

'How's Susan?' he said as Stephen walked in.

'She's very well.'

'And the baby?'

'He's fine. We called him after my father.'

'I sent you a copy of your mother's will, since you're the executor and main beneficiary.'

'I was surprised and pleased, relieved if you like. I didn't think she was going to leave me a penny.'

'The other things in the will are very ordinary, a few bequests and people remembered whom she thought should be. There was only one thing that I was surprised about, she left something to Matthew.'

'She seemed to take to him at the anniversary party and he was out of reason kind to her.'

'It doesn't bother you, then.'

'Should it? It's only an item of jewellery, isn't it? I can hardly accuse him of trying to take money after all he's done, and it's not as if he's desperate for a ... what is it, a silver locket? It can't be very valuable?'

'No, I don't suppose so.'

'I don't remember her wearing it, or that there was anything special about it. He's welcome to it. Are there going to be any problems with the will?'

'Not as far as I can see. It will take some time, of course, but the estate is worth quite a sum and it comes to you almost intact.'

'It'll be very welcome.'

'You deserve it,' Sam said. 'You did a great deal for your parents.'

'Shall I send Matthew the locket?'

'Doesn't he come to the pit?'

'Not since the anniversary party. I hear that he sold the cottage ... and Alex has sold her house.'

The package came to Matthew's house in London by special courier. He knew what it was the second he opened it. He hadn't seen it for a long time. It was his last childhood memory of her, when she had left him there in the middle of the kitchen floor at the Elliot house, she had got down to him and the locket had been around her neck.

He tore the packaging away, opened the box, pushed aside the material which covered it and there was the locket. It was smaller than he remembered, and the chain which held it was thin, as though it had been the biggest gesture of a poor man. It was oval and had markings in decoration on one side and, when he held it up, it spun around in his fingers as though it had been twisted in the box. He knocked open the catch and there inside was a curl of a child's hair.

She had looked him in the eyes and said, 'I'll come back for you, Mattie.'

All he had been able to manage was, 'When?'

'Very soon.'

'Tomorrow?' Even tomorrow was a long time when you were three, it meant that you had to stay overnight with people you didn't know. He had never done that before.

'No, not tomorrow.'

'When?'

She didn't answer that, and she had got up and started to walk away and he had cried and run after her. Somebody had picked him up and held him back and he had fought but the outside door had shut and she was gone. He had waited for her to come back for him every single day, but she never had.

Alex came into the room just as he would have secreted the locket into the desk drawer but it was too late. She had seen it shining in the sunlight.

'What's that?' she said.

'Nothing.' He sat with the locket in his fingers. It seemed silly and clumsy now to put it into the desk.

She looked closely at it.

'Not your taste?'

'No.' And then he said with an effort, 'My father bought it for my mother.'

'Really?' Alex took the locket, opened it. 'Baby hair. Is that yours? What a nice idea.'

He said nothing. Alex gave the locket to him and he put it into the desk drawer. She said clearly, 'I haven't told any of your secrets to anyone.'

'I know.'

'But you trust me with them?'

'We have a lot in common. I always think you understand.'

Alex stood for a second and then she said, 'I didn't love Tom at all. It was only because I was afraid. I didn't want to belong to anybody. I hadn't seen a successful relationship.

356

In my family nobody stayed with anybody and I was determined not to be dumped like my mother. I have to be the first to leave always, the first not to care. It's such a petty, mean way to behave but I can't help it. I wish I could go back now and marry Andrew. I do so want to do all those stupid things like making cakes and planning gardens.'

'I still think of you with Andrew in that appalling house–'

'It was not an appalling house.'

'It was a disaster and the people next door had stone lions.'

'You are such a snob,' she said, laughing. 'There is nothing wrong with lions or gnomes or anything else that people like. In your case, this is inverted snobbery, fear of ending up with stone lions in your own garden. You had orange flowers in your garden at the cottage, and that is the height of indelicacy, I will have you know!'

She was close. Matthew put both hands around her waist and pulled her down on to his knee. She waited. For a long time he didn't say anything and then, 'Mrs West was my mother. I think my father died. I don't remember him, just that he gave her the locket. I don't even know whether they were married. She was a farm girl, we lived in an isolated cottage up on the fell. I don't know how she met Ted West, but either he didn't want me or she didn't dare to tell him that she had a child. She gave the Elliots money, five pound notes, and then she left me. She never acknowledged me again, not even when I saw her the last time at the pit anniversary.'

'I see,' Alex said and then, slowly, looking him in the eyes, she said, 'Are you proposing ever to have a good relationship with a woman?'

'Are you implying that it's my fault?'

She raised her eyebrows.

'I think you probably always scupper it. Don't you?'

'Possibly.'

'But you think you might give this a try?'

'I thought I might.' He was looking past her. 'But then I thought maybe you wouldn't, because you might want to have children.'

Alex hesitated.

'I'm not your usual style. Have you ever slept with anybody who had a brain?'

He laughed.

'You do love me though?'

'Yes, I do love you. I think it has more to do with your ability to make bacon sandwiches than anything else, but it's definitely love.'

He managed to look at her.

'Will you marry me?'

'Yes,' Alex said.

Sam left his office and went through to where Caroline was working.

'Can I ask you something?'

She looked up.

'If you have half an hour, would you come to the antique shop across the marketplace with me? I want you to see these birds. I'd like your opinion.'

'Now?'

'If you can manage it. It is almost lunch-time.'

She put on her jacket and they walked up the hill and through the narrow street and across the marketplace into what Caroline felt sure was the world's most exciting antiques shop. It had always been in the town, as far as she could remember, and it held treasures, mysteries. It was a series of small rooms, up tiny stairs which seemed to twist around, and everywhere there were pieces of the past.

Some of them were small and valuable and in glass cases, and some of them were big and valuable and sat in windows, and it was all wood and must and shine, the polished

Victorian and Edwardian tables, the spindly legs on old chairs, the smell of cracked leather from various seats, and paintings and photographs of people long dead, and jewellery which had belonged on fingers which had been warm long ago.

There were amber and rubies and diamonds in rings and bracelets and necklaces and brooches, and sketches of castles in the area or photographs in sepia. There were ornaments and Indian relics and cabinets with keys and, to one side of the ground floor, there was a big sideboard, rather like the one in Sam's office, and on it stood two birds in blue and white, the blue so delicate that it could only just be distinguished from the white.

They were not the same, of course, but they had about them the same air, the same grace, the same idea – that, at any given second, should Sam choose to open his office window, they would change from china to bright eyes and warm feathers and real purpose and they would swoop past him through the open window and then they would fly high across the rooftops, making their way clear and clean towards the heather.

'Oh, Sam, they're beautiful.'

'You like them?'

'I think they're perfect. They're probably horribly expensive.'

Sam didn't seem to care. He bought them, they were wrapped carefully and boxed and then he carried them out of the shop and across the square.

'Let's go to the pub,' he said.

Caroline was suddenly hungry and they went in and it was fun. The pub had plenty of people in it, though they found a table, and everybody was talking like mad and they all knew Sam and when they hailed him he introduced her. Caroline wasn't used to feeling a part of things and she liked it. Sam bought her Theakston's beer and a beef and horseradish sandwich.

After they sat down, she thought that Sam was more than usually quiet, but she was happy just to be there in that congenial atmosphere. After a few minutes, Sam said to her, 'Would you...?' and then stopped. 'I thought you might like to come out to the farm some time.' And then he looked at her. 'This is very awkward. I don't want you to feel as though–'

She stopped him there. She put a hand on his arm and smiled and said, 'Sam, I would love to.'

'You would? Only...'

'This is the first time I've ever seen you stuck for words.'

'You were so very much in love with Stephen.'

'Perhaps I needed to be in love with somebody. It isn't Stephen I miss, it's Michael. I thought I could have Michael back, but you can't go back, you can only go forward, and there was nowhere to go with Stephen. Can I come to lunch?'

'Anything you like,' Sam said.

'I told you Sam Browne was the man for you,' her mother said triumphantly before she went off on her mystery trip.

The Saturday was bright and fine. Like a good many other people, Caroline always wanted to keep on going through the white gates when she got to Sam's house. The road wound into an S bend there, which had to be negotiated, and it was therefore impossible to catch more than a glimpse of the ruins, or the house itself, so it was particularly satisfying to keep on going through the open gates and up to the buildings. She half expected dogs to come out and meet her, they usually did in farmyards, but none did, only a black and white cat which looked on curiously from some distance away. Sam's house was very like his office, the furniture was old and used and there were lots of bookshelves, bulging with books. There were paintings on the walls and plain carpets with patterned rugs on the floors and the windows were small because the building was old. There was an open fire in the big sitting room, and squashy sofas. Lamps were lit in the rooms. Gardens sloped away towards fields, lawns and flower beds.

He gave her a glass of white wine which tasted of vanilla and gooseberries and they ate smoked salmon and cream-cheese parcels, chicken in tarragon with cream sauce and new potatoes and green beans, and a lemon pudding. They had coffee by the fire and then they looked around outside before the light was gone. There were byres and barns, a chicken coop, a paddock, a pond – it had everything, but the place she liked most was the ruined castle.

'Does it have a history?'

'People have lived on this spot since the eighth century, Scandinavian settlement, a lot of fighting on both sides of the border later, and on the same side sometimes. Apparently a sixteenth-century bishop who was a religious martyr was born here. He was burned at the stake at Oxford.'

'It sounds hideous,' Caroline said.

From the castle, when you had been able to climb to the top, you would have been able to see for miles around, to make sure that your enemies were way out of sight before you went back to the house.

There were sheep and cattle in the fields. A pheasant ran across the path and in the stillness of the afternoon a few snowflakes fell. There was a burn which tumbled over stones and down towards a small bridge across the road further over, and the sun set in a blaze of gold and grey. They went back and drank tea by the fire.

Caroline was reluctant to go. It was Saturday, supposedly the best night of the week, and she had nobody to go home to, but she did not want Sam to think she was presuming anything. He walked her to her car and when they got to it he said, 'Would you like to go out with me tomorrow? This is difficult–'

'It isn't difficult. I would very much like to go out with you, Sam,' and she leaned over and kissed him on the cheek.

'Are you sure?'

'Certain. Did you have somewhere in mind?'

'I thought maybe a long wide beach.'

'That would be perfect,' Caroline said.

'Do you have to go back now?'

'No. No, I don't.'

Sam took her into his arms and kissed her. It wasn't like kissing Stephen, but it was just as good, and it wasn't like kissing Michael and she couldn't remember whether it was as good, and that was a step forward, she thought. They walked slowly back towards the house and, for the first time since Michael had died, Caroline felt a small degree of contentment. She wasn't sure whether it would last, but she was very keen to give it a try.

The publishers hope that this book has given you enjoyable reading. Large Print Books are especially designed to be as easy to see and hold as possible. If you wish a complete list of our books please ask at your local library or write directly to:

Magna Large Print Books
Magna House, Long Preston,
Skipton, North Yorkshire.
BD23 4ND

This Large Print Book, for people
who cannot read normal print,
is published under the auspices of

THE ULVERSCROFT FOUNDATION